Qwert and the Wedding Gown

QWERT
and the
Wedding Gown

by
Matías Montes Huidobro

Translated by John Mitchell and
Ruth Mitchell de Aguilar

Plover Press
Kaneohe, Hawaii
1992

Printed and Bound in the United States of America

Design by Paula Newcomb
Cover Illustration by Mirta Toledo

Library of Congress Cataloging-in-Publication Data

Montes Huidobro, Matías
    [Desterrados al fuego. English]
    Qwert and the wedding gown / Matías Montes Huidobro ;
translated by John Mitchell and Ruth Mitchell de Aguilar.
        p.   cm.
    Translation of : Desterrados al fuego.
    ISBN 0-917635-12-4 : $18.95. — ISBN 0-917635-13-2 : $9.95
    I. Title.
PQ7390.M65D413   1992
863—dc20   92-6005
                                                               CIP

Distributed by
The Talman Company, Inc.
150 Fifth Avenue
New York, NY 10011

A Yara,
todo y siempre

CHAPTER

1

We don't know at exactly what point during our trip we began to experience those peculiar changes. I remember that Amanda used to say that everything began when we left our country without being able to take our possessions with us. The government had strict rules and you were not able to take more than three changes of clothing. From the beginning this was a hard decision to make because we were going to have to get along with these few belongings in a foreign country for some time. The decision had to be considered with utmost care, and since we didn't have much to do until the government deigned to give us permission to leave (which sometimes took years), we spent long hours in front of our wardrobe, deciding if we would take this or that. We had to leave many things behind.

In reality the importance of this matter was relative. Our home was modest and the government was not going to end up with any great fortune. Consequently, more than being saddened by the material loss, it was really the spiritual deprivation that hurt. Among our possessions there were two things it was painful to leave behind: Amanda's wedding dress and my typewriter.

1

When we were married we made a decision never to abandon that wedding dress. Many young people, in the middle class particularly, rent a wedding dress for the ceremony, or sell theirs afterwards. We were determined never to do this, neither the one nor the other, on account of the spiritual importance we placed on the matter. Unfortunately, we didn't anticipate the political changes that were going to come later, and the dress also had to be left behind. The typewriter, naturally, had a less sentimental character, but since I was intellectually linked to it through my ambitions as a writer, particularly as a novelist, the separation from it was also something painful. In spite of everything, we made a last-ditch effort to save these things from strange hands. We sent them for safekeeping to a town in the interior where my mother lived. Someone, nevertheless, reported the arrival of the suspicious baggage and it was confiscated. My mother made efforts to recover it, and the valise which had contained the dress did come back to her, although not the typewriter, which until this day is probably working reliably in some cramped corner, printing military orders or who knows what awful denunciations. I doubt that its tasks are fictional. With regard to the wedding dress, we don't know the nature of its fate. We imagine that it underwent rigorous alterations and that it was never used in another wedding.

The remainder of what was left behind meant much less to us. Amanda complained for a while about the loss of a bedroom set (with which she planned to die, she used to say) and indulged in the illusory act of locking the doors of the closet wardrobe and taking the keys with her, thereby obliging those who got it to force the lock. No doubt they did so. The keys, that we still have somewhere, have turned enough and it's possible as uselessly as we have ourselves. The fate of the bedroom set has ceased to matter to us, and certainly it gives us a certain peace of mind to know that neither Amanda nor I will die in that bed.

We were hoping, certainly, that such losses would have no special significance in our lives. But of this more later.

The decision with respect to the three changes of clothes appeared to have little importance, although it was not without a certain interest. It was my position that the type of clothes we took would determine the place we were going to live. If we decided on winter clothing, possibly we would go toward the north, where we would have the opportunity of using it, while if we only took summer clothes, we would have to opt for a region with a warm climate more like our own and one generally preferred by the other emigrants. Amanda was scandalized by such an absurd idea and said I was crazy. Her assertion was logical: one didn't go to a place according to the clothes that he had, but dressed according to the places where he went. The fact that we carried this type of clothing or that was not going to affect our final decision of going north or remaining in the south. Besides, one could acquire adequate clothing for a cold climate even if he decided in favor of a tropical wardrobe. I made bold to argue that if we had no money (we were already banned from taking a cent out of the country), it was not going to be possible to buy new clothes, an opinion which Amanda contradicted by asserting that one earned money by working. It was clear that her explanation was logical; nevertheless, I was still doubtful and thought that at least we ought to take a sweater. Eventually I came to think that Amanda was right.

In any case, all that seemed pretty minor. What did a change of clothes more or less matter when your whole life was at stake? Besides, those who stayed behind would also have to suffer privations (as time has proven) and adjust themselves to all that we had left. This argument, according to Amanda, was not very consoling since those who remained would have the advantage of acquiring things that never would have been within their reach were it not for the exodus. I told her that it was not possible that a humble field worker (from Bejucal, for example) would ever feel comfortable living in the ancient residence of an aristocratic family and that the maladjustment would be evident and would end up making him feel wretched. Amanda laughed at me again, saying that as far as the worker's being out of place was concerned I was right, but not in the matter of being unlucky. True, in a certain sense it was going to be a mismatch, an anachronism, but he would feel his hour of glory had come.

These conversations went on for hours. Since at that time they weren't sending people who wanted to leave the country out into the fields at forced labor, we had to pass the time doing something or go crazy in the midst of the desperation and tedium. This last idea, the imbalance that would be produced between people and things, began to make my head swim, and were it not for the hard fact of losing the typewriter it's possible that in that moment I might have written a novel. Which indicated, I thought, that a simple circumstance (the absence of a typewriter) was enough to distance me fatally from the temple of fame. How was it possible that Amanda could be so sure that we would go northward if all we carried was light summer wear? But in general everything seemed inevitable, as if part of the historical process within which we found ourselves.

The truth was that those three changes of clothing that accompanied us on our departure would not make much difference. In the first place they were insufficient, not to mention the fact that ours would be completely out of style. This last was a minor detail (like all the rest), but

4

from the beginning it marked us in a peculiarly contradictory way, integrating us with a group while at the same
time isolating us from the rest—which was by far the vast
majority. Thus one became a member of a class (the
group), but ceased being part of the larger world. We were,
basically, excluded. This identification with the group (the
group of recent arrivals, to be exact, those in the most
straitened circumstances) was basically negative. Because
the idea grows more and more marked in the consciousness of exiles that "we are all not equal." Our manner of
dressing, archaic, obsolete, made us appear a little odd, as
if we came from a foreign planet. Of course, we were not
alone. Those who were in the same category with us felt
particularly set up when they saw us dressed in the same
way that they still were. They thought that we belonged
to them when they saw the discolored cotton print of
Amanda's modest dress, ironed and ironed again until it
was somewhat shiny, and the no less discolored blue shirt
that I always wore and that at times seemed to be an
integral part of my body.

This frequent hobnobbing set loose in me a vague and
growing predilection I had never experienced before,
toward filth. I had always been moderately tidy, never
going to the extreme of exaggerated neatness, but never
becoming disagreeably dirty either. I complied with my
hygienic duties in the proper way, although it is fair to
say without enthusiasm. I bathed every day (save for those
winter days when I opted to omit it), I brushed my teeth
on getting up and after each meal, used deodorant to avoid
the disagreeable smell of sweat (which my compatriots
classify crudely as the *stink of the great unwashed*) and
changed my clothing regularly, particularly in the case of
my underwear and socks. These last acquired an especially
disagreeable odor if I didn't change them sufficiently
often, and my relatives on my mother's side, carried by

5

an exaggerated nationalism, liked to say that it (BO) was a Spanish trait. The guilt fell, therefore, on my father. This tendency was no great bother for me, but for others it caused considerable inconvenience. Amanda, who was the acme of cleanliness, was very conscious of such an organic deficiency and always had at hand the requisite medicinal talcs. Finally, although I was a little careless of dress, after our marriage Amanda dedicated herself so much to the modification of this unfortunate trait in my character that the obvious improvement in my appearance won some unmerited praise from our most refined friends.

Nevertheless, the beneficial influence did not extend to the shoes. I rarely resorted to a bootblack and I could not be counted on to go and sit in one of those ostentatious chairs (a species of grotesque throne, under the dirty tropical arcades) where the bootblacks did their priestly work and our more typical citizens preened themselves, acting like birds of feather. That cult of patent leather brilliance or the sexually doubtful filigree of two-tone shoes was never in vogue with me. Sometimes, against my better judgment, I would give in to the pressures of my environment and timidly solicit the services of some humble negro shoeshine boy, such as abound in Central Park, accepting the implicit discomfort of his inhuman box. I consoled myself with the thought that it was all in the nature of a public service. The luster was merely transitory and my hygienic constancy (in that sense) operated in inverse proportion to the constancy of the dust. The disagreeable things that I had in reach of my hand at home, such as shoe polish, brushes, cloth for making the shoes shine, only had a temporary effect, and their use required a constant pressure that went beyond Amanda's capacity for insistence. For beyond discipline, good intentions, periodic repentence and proposals to mend my ways the persistent habit of uncleanliness had taken root.

Perhaps it was a matter of seeking a means of genuine self-expression through the last redoubt of the feet. Undoubtedly it threw into relief a trait that must be called atypical since the shine on the shoes (and in general every hygienic manifestation) are national characteristics. My compatriots were (I am not sure if they still are, given the significant political changes which have taken place) extremely cleanly. Climatological conditions (the tropical heat) incline one toward frequent baths and bodily hygiene is obligatory. One sweats, certainly, but never lacks the refreshing evening bath. It was a country rich in bath soaps, colognes, deodorants and other toilet products, a contradiction of the general concept of an undeveloped country. Perfumes were used with moderation and never (as they say of the French) as a superstructure for bad odor. To do such a thing was an absolute breach of etiquette. The men boasted well-cut hair and the fortnightly visit to the barbershop was a fact of life. Men typically wore a conservative moustache, and the five o'clock shadow was insistently pursued as if the beard itself were a danger. And the most extreme manifestation of our racism was to affirm that the negroes smelled different—the euphemism is mine. Except for the Gentleman of Paris (and note again the chauvinism of our national consciousness) it had occurred to no one (in those times) to rebel through grime. I certainly didn't count myself among such renegades in the making and limited myself to those critical signs of the feet, whether they be internal attributes of the Basque genes of my father or the external product of my civil disobedience.

The impatient reader must not believe that this insistence of mine on the feet will result in a difficult digression that takes me from my theme. In no way; completely the reverse. I have thought many times that this background is necessary to comprehend the things that would happen to me later, especially in the matter of the overcoat. I understand, nevertheless, that I ought not to delay the story and at the same time not anticipate it overly. I'm not trying to make a political question of this either, and if I have advanced some idea in relation to our national characteristics it is because of the close relation they have with the experiences that have befallen me and the medium within which said experiences have unfolded. Many of these thoughts were born of the difficult analysis inherent in my circumstances.

So far as Amanda goes, I will only add (regarding these aspects I plan to treat) that she was typical in the extreme in matters of personal hygiene and that one of the great crises prior to our exile took place when, fearful that the lack of soap would be a certainty and frightened at the force of her own logic, she began hiding cakes of bath soap inside the plaster lamps that we had in the living and dining rooms. The obsession (very similar to Ray Milland's in the *The Last Weekend*, a title I think I have wrong) seemed to point toward a no less traumatic and tragic conclusion, especially the day we discovered that the bars, thanks to a shadow created by the light bulb, caused pantomime shapes to appear on the ceiling. The decline of filth is a matter of history, and its national rejection gave rise among counterrevolutionaries to the heavy nickname "bola de churre" or ball of filth. For reasons of public and private hygiene our departure from the homeland was imminent.

This places us again (thank God) in a foreign land, a place we had arrived some pages back. We have noted that the clothing created an immediate feeling of belonging and familiarity among those who were in similar circumstances (the group within the group), producing at the same time a rapid ejection by those who, having cast aside their discolored apparel, had had the opportunity to acquire clothing more in keeping with the current mode. The effect was multiple. On the one hand we were accepted socially by those less fortunate, although we were in no way respected by them. At bottom each one (of us) wanted to break out of the group to which he belonged in order to hobnob with those who had succeeded in advancing themselves. We pretended to scorn those on the next rung, but at the same time there was no doubt that we would have preferred to be in their place. I include myself in those assertions I make because not to would be discourteous, petulant and vain. Certainly it would not be ethical.

The above tendency bred resentment and jealousy among the immigrants. All, sooner or later, had chosen exile, but the very act created distinctions of every character. I told Amanda that it reminded me of the business of the beards, that some by affecting longer whiskers believed they were somehow more potent than others. Resentment, then, was our daily bread. Some persons had had no luck (or had preferred not to have it) and for years had had to wear that discolored apparel they had brought with them. The colors, as is natural, had faded day after day, and especially blue (a color that for obvious reasons easily makes one seasick) evolved in a doubtful way toward green, creating occasions for long and tortuous disputes about the original color of the article in question.

These garments deteriorated even faster because of the ancient concept of hygiene to which we have already alluded. In my opinion (and this is an opinion acquired from years of experience) soap not only produces a marked deterioration in textiles, but also in the body. But as the reasons for the mass exodus had overtones in the personal hygiene which formed one of the dominant routines on our island, including a marked rejection of filth and the dirtiness of the regime in power, the typical evidences of cleanliness were put on display with more vigor than ever, in a form that was paradoxical in a civilization that was (say what you will) less cleanly, but more advanced! It was a matter of conscience that nothing or no one should stink, and that the modest, humble articles of clothing were always immaculately clean (often darned and covered with patches) and ironed, although laughably worn out.

Both Amanda and I felt uncomfortable in the midst of that environment in which the enmities of the emigrés increased day by day and from which the vanity of hygiene was never far. It would be best, we decided, to move on, to remain where we were the least possible time. We had begun our peregrination and did not want anything to stop us. Would our expulsion turn into a constant journey with changes of housing and search for baggage? Our first contacts were so disagreeable that I began to think that it would be better to find a home in the happy company of airports and amidst the obsequious smiles of stewardesses.

Our thought was that more to the north life would be different and the people, possibly, not quite so bad. The situation was growing worse and worse. Some didn't want to accept as "theirs" (equal but separate) those who had arrived last, dressed of course in ways that were even more outlandish. The concept of "the last one's a rotten tomato," infantile to be sure, was put into practice. Out of it grew a new social class among the first arrivals (who were now considered old) that tried to distinguish itself by means of rings, watches, chains, and other articles that must have a certain number of carats.

Amanda's situation was, in a certain sense, worse than mine. I should say that Amanda had a natural elegance that was always present, that flowed from her person without premeditation or artifice. This fact is of particular importance because it was not going to be realized during that period we will call "the difficult time of the overcoat," which gave some measure of how terrible our future circumstances would be. Because of this flare, when Amanda put on her worn-out faded cotton dress, something showed through from underneath that humble vestment which evoked the clothing she no longer wore. This made her suspect, as if she were not, indeed, "part of the group." Years later (that perhaps we will never mention) this characteristic was going to cause Amanda problems when someone invited her to a party and said, "Come however you wish," in this way making it impossible for her to find the proper clothing. She always went formally dressed. In these first days of exile the situation was even worse because Amanda had had the impractical idea of bringing two changes of fancy clothes, one which would make her look well (or different) in circumstances where quite the contrary might have been preferable. My destiny was to appear somewhat unkempt, a quality which was balanced by Amanda's innate distinction. Although I dressed badly in my own way (which was atypical), I don't know if it ever produced any positive result.

At first Amanda's fine attire permitted her certain temporary contacts that lasted until they saw me (who very definitely had brought only one change of good clothes that had rapidly ceased being that, thanks to my habitual carelessness), and they began criticizing her for taking the "misstep" of marrying me. And it was not because they wished her ill; on the contrary, it was because they were unable to accept the social anachronism we represented. How had a girl like Amanda married an individual that never cleaned his shoes and was less than agreeable, plus being a little obtuse. There is no doubt that they weren't acting from malice and that they felt a clear sympathy for her, but the conclusion was inevitable. If Amanda had been alone, her fate might have been otherwise since my unfortunate manners wouldn't have been detrimental to her.

Consequently our situation was bound to worsen with the passage of time since we found no work (the competition was tremendous and a little hateful) and already the deterioration of our clothing was well advanced. My shoes (by the way, they only allowed us to take one pair) were in deplorable condition—and I don't refer to the theme of dust and shine, but to the irremediable wear of the soles that had all the appearances of a catastrophe. Amanda's good dresses continued going downhill and proved their worthlessness (they were not going to feed us) in the sphere of "the group outside the group," *elite* who preferred to trip you up to reduce the competition; and her clothing in turn occasioned the rejection among the rabble or "the group within the group" (who were also not going to resolve anything, however they might want to). What sense was there in remaining in a place where the emigrés themselves devoured each other within a framework of petty quarrels, adding envy to other festering wounds? It was necessary to leave.

Again the difficult problem of clothing presented itself. I had always feared it. Immediately the comments began. Everyone had an opinion to give and no solutions to offer. "I wanted to go but didn't have anything to wear," said some, and were satisfied with that simple justification. "If one doesn't have a good overcoat and all the trappings, he'll end by catching pneumonia," said others, with a logic that appeared more realistic to me. "It's crazy! But where do you think you're going to go?" "You'll never get there; many have died en route," said those with more fantastic imaginations. "The cold is brutal. But is it that you don't understand it's like living in Siberia?" "Many have returned." "Those were the lucky ones, because those that weren't have died in hospitals and are rotting in frozen cemeteries," returned the more tragic and metaphorical. All the opinions were macabre. "It's strange," said an old man who took the sun every morning in Dove Park, "here in exile many people are paralyzed. Including some who have crossed the sea by boat, thumbing their noses at the Coast Guard and risking their very lives. They make a big decision and leave everything, but now they're afraid to move."

Amanda agreed that was the worst: the paralysis. If it was bad to die of pneumonia in one of those impersonal hospitals of dark bricks where no relative was able to keep us company, under an immensity of sunless gray sky, it was worse to remain paralyzed in a shabby room in a southern ghetto, completely forgotten by all, hearing the incessant scampering of rats through the empty halls and waiting for the heart to cease once and for all. Letters unanswered, bills unpaid, the stench finding its way through walls and windows until finally some pious soul would call the police who, complying with the requirements of an efficient community, would end by throwing us in a common grave in some southern cemetery. At any rate, I argued that we didn't have the necessary clothing and that obtaining it was the first step we had to take if we wanted to undertake a trip.

It wasn't true that it was so difficult to leave. The alarming accounts merely confirmed the principle of paralysis in which many were submerged. One somewhat older gentleman, though not old, a professional with a certain reputation, finally spoke to us as follows: "Really, I'm afraid to travel and the only reason I've come so far is to avoid the terrible conditions which have seized our country. Travel terrifies me, especially by sea, since there is no guaranteeing nowadays we'll reach our destination. I don't believe that a world exists 'out there,' and I'm sure that

13

all this news which appears in the press at present is an invention to make us believe that the world is larger than it is and to get us to leave where we are. What proof do we have that beyond the horizon there doesn't exist a deep abyss where the boats sink and the land ends in a precipice enveloped in flames that devour us?" "But some people come back and say nothing of this," I dared to suggest. "Don't believe any of them. They're agents. I'm not moving from here." Amanda and I looked at each other in astonishment, not because of what that man was telling us, but because he was saying it at all. It was essential that we persist in our plans. The procedure was fairly simple and the government (which had an office to aid emigrés) was in favor of relocation. It paid for the tickets and provided the necessary wardrobe for conquering the winter.

The clothing was not, as was to be expected, in the latest style. A Protestant agency was in charge of furnishing wearing apparel for exiles. An agreeable matron with a light impersonal touch took care of us. She herself appeared to be wearing clothes from the agency: a gray dress, straight-cut (with a belt sewn at the waist so that the hips were not defined, as if covered like an ironing board), long sleeves—it wrapped her "vividly" from neck to knees. There was an abundance of clothing, but it was hard to find anything that was halfway acceptable. It appeared as though the items had been deliberately selected to make you look bad before the world. The overcoats had been good, of pure wool, dark colors, but they showed the passage of time as if they had been supplied to us twenty years ago. More, perhaps. We felt we were in the "Charleston" era. In the midst of the fitting Amanda seemed to lose her strength. Slowly but surely a great weakness came over her, as if she were in the clutches of a wild beast. She, so bold and decided in preferring to die of pneumonia if it was necessary, but not of paralysis (conclusions in which Amanda saw considerable differences), was overcome by the weight of those woolen overcoats there in the contaminated atmosphere of a storage room which produced a kind of asphyxia. The matron, somewhat put out because we couldn't make up our minds, made unlikely suggestions about how well this overcoat would suit us, or that one—"as if it was made to order for you," she said so often and so thoughtlessly that we began to think she was being sarcastic. She wasn't. She simply wanted to close up and leave for home, knowing that no matter how many things we tried on we were still going to look the same since that institution was made up of hand-me-downs. Certainly another couple of our same age (the woman attractively young and elegant and her companion a skinny, awkward type) saw themselves reflected in some overcoats of worn-out rabbit skins which made them look killingly bad. Nevertheless, they kept them and smiled at us from the mirror as if they had wisely hit the mark with their decision. Perhaps it was for that reason we finally made up our minds (we had to do it sooner or later anyway), although I'm afraid we chose the worst. Amanda selected a black formless overcoat that was too broad for her and so long it almost reached her ankles. "At least," she said, to console herself, "I will be protected from the cold." I decided on another that in its time must have been of the finest quality, although such indications seemed prehistoric. A cockroach had eaten the boarder off one sleeve, and the collar, of a grotesque and pretentious velvet, had rough circular spots where there wasn't a trace of the pre-existent pile.

The consequences of this first decision were going to prove all but fatal, and who knows if we will ever recover completely. Arriving at our flat, we hung the coats in an unused closet, with the intention of not looking at them

15

again until the very moment of parting. In fact, Amanda was so depressed that as soon as she was able to recover from the impact occasioned by that exertion, she began telling me that maybe the others were right and that perhaps it would be better to remain here in the hope that some change in the political situation would permit us to return to our country. She fell short only in failing to reaffirm the theory of oceanic abysses or that we would end being devoured by sea serpents. But I knew that Amanda was saying all this because of the overcoat, and it must have been a worse shock to her since she had an authentic concept of elegance which I lacked. Although I was suddenly less sure of things myself, I told her we should not allow ourselves to be carried away by our first setback. "What do you call our first setback?" she asked me, knowing perfectly well what I meant. "The overcoat." "The overcoats, you mean," Amanda corrected. "Actually, that's what I mean." On being made to face the situation directly, she understood it was clearly ridiculous. Are we going to let ourselves be thrown off by a pair of overcoats? Are we going to let some overcoats determine the course of our lives? Who ever heard of such a thing? Amanda said all this in a loud voice because in reality she wished to convince herself. According to her, we had to be strong to overcome adversity. Hadn't we left behind really important things? And she thought possibly of the wedding dress from which she never wished to part. Or the bedroom set, much more personal and familiar than an unknown hospital bed. I didn't say anything because it had really been she who had cast the question in a negative light. She said then that we ought to face up to things and went to the closet and took out the overcoats. She returned holding the two coats from hangers, and the image she cast struck me as terrible, as though she had two black wings. Fortunately there were no mirrors in the apartment. Otherwise Amanda would have died.

She insisted then that we try on the overcoats. We had to accustom ourselves to seeing ourselves with them on. I tried to get out of it, but she insisted. The apartment was hermetically sealed and the atmosphere was charged. Amanda put hers on and I mine. Soon she said, looking at me strangely, as if she saw right through me: "Come in, come in. Don't just stand there in the door. You're going to freeze." I turned around because it appeared she wasn't talking to me, but evidently she was, for there was no one there. "Come in, come in. Don't just stand there in the door. You're going to freeze," she repeated, adding in a way that struck me as somewhat vulgar: "You've got to warm up." And presently she said, as if someone had said something: "And how was I to know? I'm going to make you a cup of coffee." Amanda went toward the little table-top stove, which was partially hidden on one side of the apartment and which I naturally had never noticed. She opened the faucet in the washstand that was near her, filled a little earthenware pot with water, and after lighting the stove with a match turned to me.

Suffice it to say that all this was occurring in an imaginary realm, because the apartment was a poor thing (our room, I mean), and she was pretending it wasn't. Nevertheless, when she turned toward me, the perspective changed completely, and I felt strongly that to react as though this scene were real, or to prolong it, would lead us God knows where. She looked at me with a certain foreboding even, as if she feared me, as if at any moment I was going to take out a dagger (like Jack the Ripper) and do away with her. A strange force was taking possession of me and she was powerless to escape it. Did she see me perhaps as someone she had met in the park and whom, imprudently, she had invited to our apartment?

But that scenario, coming from Amanda, who was so suspicious of people, was completely inadmissible. Maybe it was because I had not taken off the overcoat, but kept it on in spite of the asphyxiating atmosphere that existed in the apartment, that she became convinced that the man she saw had a dagger hidden in his pocket. Actually, my hand was paralyzed in the overcoat pocket and I couldn't predict what I was going to do with it. Weren't assaults part of our daily life and the stabbing of women what enriched press headlines every morning? All this possibly, occurred in the space of an instant, and although I wasn't conscious of what I might do from one moment to the next, it ended with my doing nothing. Amanda continued looking at me horrified, and I found myself unable to move so as to calm her and tell her it was I. My own name sounded hollow in my ears. Then she, without being able to contain herself, launched herself at me, focusing on the arm, which she yanked from the pocket of the overcoat to prove that I didn't have a knife in my hand. She was on the point of collapsing on the floor.

As best I could, I shed the overcoat and threw it on an armchair while almost carrying her to the bed, where I let her drop. She was ghastly pale and her pallor was accentuated by the black overcoat, which reached almost to her feet. I'm not sure, but I think she lost consciousness. She was completely loose at the joints, her face disfigured, her mouth contorted as if all life (everyone's life) had passed through her in that moment. As best I could, I removed her overcoat. Little by little she appeared to recover. She opened her eyes as if she came from very far away and did not remember where she had been, and she smiled at me—was it that she finally recognized me? Then she said that she was very tired and wished to sleep. Immediately she fell asleep in a way that was tranquil and relaxed, but very profound.

I continued thinking of the matter and, in spite of what had happened, I told myself it was necessary to rise above such apprehensions. That is to say, above the overcoat. Let me be absolutely clear, since I fear that I may have misled the reader into thinking this is one of those cases that lie somewhere between a detective story and a fantasy in which the victims suffer from a curse that comes from something they wear. Certainly something very strange had taken place, although not as strange as the other things that were happening to us and in the face of which we didn't react half so dramatically. For example, the predicament of having to live with the three changes of clothing that we brought into exile. In that moment I realized that whatever was the truth regarding the overcoats was also true with respect to my discolored cotton shirts, the faded print of Amanda's cotton dress, or the formal attire (now completely out of style) she continued using in spite of the dissonant effect it created. It was evident that if we remained here, we would end in the most frightening paralysis, and that the true danger of the overcoats lay in our fear, in our cowardice in not wishing to confront the situation that lay ahead.

This argument struck me with less force when I looked at the overcoats and saw myself—consciously—alone before them (since Amanda was sleeping), one of them over the armchair and the other on the floor. I ought to touch them, pick them up, take care of them. No, they weren't taking on life, I told myself. Gathering all my courage, I collected them, hung them on their respective hangers, and put them in the closet. I threw myself on the bed, dressed as I was, and slept.

The next morning I made the following resolution: to go pick up the traveling money, pack the few things that we had, put on the overcoats and leave as soon as possible. And so it was. That is to say we went out to obtain tickets

19

and returned to pack our bags. After everything was ready, the moment came to confront the overcoats.

Amanda appeared to have forgotten what had happened the night before. I didn't dare remind her. Furthermore, I had to make every effort to see that something of the sort did not take place again. I took her by the hand and told her that we had to be brave because we were starting a long trip and that come what might now was the time to be more united than ever. To Amanda my way of talking seemed rather strange because of the didactic, discursive tone that was unusual in me. She said she didn't understand why I was saying all that, because I knew better than anyone that our love was proof against all perils. This was true, I told her, but it was also true that unknown dangers would threaten us. "Which ones?" was her question. I didn't know what to say. The only thing I could think of to answer was: "the overcoats."

"Don't be ridiculous," was her immediate reaction. "No, I'm not. Something strange happened last night with regard to the overcoats that I don't want to happen again." "I don't believe it. You're saying it to scare me." "No, on the contrary. If we're aware of the danger, I think we can overcome it. Last night, after you put on your overcoat, you began to scream and went into a faint. It's clear that you fear the overcoats." "Don't be a fool," and she went to the closet door with the intention of opening it. "No, don't open it now." It seemed like one of those second-rate mystery movies where someone opens the door of a closet and a body falls out. Or a comedy where the same thing occurs. Nevertheless, I took this very seriously. "I want to be absolutely sure that the overcoats don't represent a danger, that we have nothing to fear from them. Understand that they aren't ours. I mean that before they belonged to somebody else." "Don't tell me that they carry a curse." "I don't know. They simply don't suit us.

We look very bad in them." "And what's that got to do with it?" "It must mean something, but both of us are ignoring it. If you and I are united against them, nothing bad can happen. We should never be too sure of things because that certainty could be our undoing." Amanda looked at me thoughtfully, as if she understood at least part of my reasons. There might be something absurd about the surface but in the depths (inscrutable) was something extremely logical. She also understood that there was a hidden truth, a little confused, but no less a truth. "You're right, but I believe that at some point we have to open the closet."

Actually, we were already on our feet, rigid, before the door of the closet. I opened it slowly, prepared, as if expecting a wild beast to jump out. But nothing happened. There they were, the overcoats, asleep, tranquil. "We're going to touch them and not be afraid," I said, reaching out my hand toward them. I said it in a loud voice to drive away the shadow of ill omen, as when you go through open country in the dark and whistle to break the loneliness. It seemed that by verbalizing the fear I could conquer the danger. Amanda assumed a slightly different attitude (although it hid a very similar fear) and ventured a joke: "They don't seem to bite." I took hold of hers with a certain foreboding. And I held it out to her. "Touch it, but don't put it on. It's much too hot and we'd be uncomfortable in them." The excuse seemed logical. Amanda took hold of hers and passed her hand over it as though it were a slightly savage animal and she wanted to calm it and avoid a dangerous lunge. I couldn't avoid making the association. "It's pure wool," she said. Next she caressed the satin lining as if seeking a pleasant intimacy. "I don't think you'll be cold in it," I said. "Now we have to see yours," said Amanda. She took hold of it without fear (or so I thought because she didn't appear

21

to feel any) and handed me mine. "Touch it, don't be afraid. I don't think it will bite either," she said, pretending to smile. It was heavy and it was in worse condition than hers, although in better times it must have been finer. We confirmed that, in reality, it did not bite.

CHAPTER

2

As we didn't have much to do or much baggage to get ready, we arrived at the airport well ahead of time, carrying our humble and outdated cardboard suitcase, shamefully light, with our few possessions dancing inside. It's fair to say that this was our first experience with airports. The departure from our country had been made under such alarming conditions that one had less the sense of a voyage than of a pathological persecution. At the airport, however, I experienced a new sensation that was a mixture of loneliness, indifference, and emptiness that blurred the lines between good and evil and was dominated by a consciousness that was the natural consequence of the most complete and total dehumanization. I thought immediately that all the normal human assumptions were presumptuous and false.

Paradoxically, the airport also created a feeling of warm maternal welcome. I was struck immediately by its immense vault of crystal and concrete, that (despite its size) did not seem foreign. It was circular and broad, as if it could hold everything, and although its immensity accentuated our tininess it created at the same time a sense of protection against all the inclemencies of the external world, particularly nature's. The crystal and concrete, far from showing the cruel indifference of the outdoors (which I generally think of when I see a tree)—inconstant, with unpredictable ups and downs of weather not even a meteorologist can predict—gave me the sensation of something incapable of doing damage, of something secure, firm, with an absolute control of temperature and light. What serenity inside a space so perfectly created to technological perfection that protects its creatures (creatures of the airport) with the intention of sparing them some dangerous pneumonia! What insecurity when one contemplates the heavenly vault in the middle of the night (even when seen through a starry tropical sky) without knowing the exact moment when a bolt might come that rends us asunder! In no other place had I experienced anything similar, except perhaps in the memories of childhood (not in the experience itself) during those remote years when I lived on Calle Colón (now Iván Ocho) in Pinar, there in the distant days of my infancy. It was as though I had recovered the forgotten residence that I had always sought and now regained out of nowhere. Perhaps this sensation of security served to diminish the effect (generally negative) of the overcoat that I carried on my arm. What pleased me most was that nobody was going to say goodbye to us, and there wasn't the remotest possibility that anyone would meet us at the other airport. Amanda and I were there alone, and a multitude of strangers (who to make things even more perfect did not even speak our language and whose speech was almost unknown) moved hurriedly around us as if they were going somewhere. It occurred to me (in the style of that peculiar personality who anticipated the worst events in the previous chapter) that those individuals were not going anywhere and that as soon as they passed through the concourse gates they would fall into one of Dante's fiery

24

abysses. It calmed me when I saw some of those return who had gone out (for sanitary reasons, surely), and based on what I overheard I began to develop a kind of faith in the Hindu doctrine of transmigration, although I really didn't know much about it. But it must be about something, and perhaps it was about something better. In spite of this teleological (?) thought, it was not the dominant one beneath the quiet of that arch which did not offer (fortunately) any call toward the mystical. In church a frightening commotion always occurred inside me, upsetting me, and images seemed to revolve in an agonizing way within. Especially Christ. What spiritual unrest could there possibly be in those ads for cigarettes, prophylactics, luxury hotels, contraceptives, products to toast the skin like a chitterling, as well as heavenly trips to island paradises which exist only in minds attacked by malaria and in the pockets of shareholders in airline companies? An emotional freedom (that seemed totally successful) was what the controlled atmosphere produced in my spirit. Beyond that, there was no melodramatic emphasis for one who leaves or arrives (flight such and such at gate such and such at such and such an hour) and Amanda, seated rigidly at my side, nonexistent almost, was scarcely a traveling companion, in the literal sense of the word.

The absence of relatives made me remember my mother, and for a moment I was wounded by a deep nostalgia (absolutely selfish), but I managed to erase it quickly, as if it had to do with a sin written in chalk. I remembered that as a child I used to go to a school in a neighboring town and that my mother went with me every Sunday to the train station to say goodbye, and on Fridays when I returned she would be there waiting. In spite of the fact this separation was routine, the emotional impact was dramatic. Even more affecting were the trips to the capital, where I never went alone. My uncles and aunts, as well as my cousins, would go to the station platform and wave their handkerchiefs like the wings of birds (white, naturally) while our tiny heads appeared like scales on the outside of the iron serpent which was dragging us away. Literary images had always impressed me.

The memory of my mother was like a knife running through me, her absence a wound, as if her body rested in the depths of my consciousness. And yet the absence of my mother in the airport gave me a sensation of security in my loneliness (or in our loneliness, now that Amanda was with me) that I wouldn't have been able to feel had my mother been present. In spite of this absence, in the infinite or indefinite atmosphere of the airport there was something as remote and sheltering as a nest. The immense building welcomed me as it did the others, buds in constant motion, without showing a trace of unfair preference for anyone. It had the absolute democratic and egalitarian conscience of an ideal Father who accepts all offerings with an equal sympathy. That profound sense of justice was what the people (in their stupid, farcical, pseudohumanitarianism) sought to classify as impersonal and dehumanized.

With respect to the others, I felt completely isolated, as though they projected like images from a movie screen. The distance was even greater, since in the movies there exists the possibility of interaction with the drama and the hero, while here the absolute ignorance of those beings and their rapid passage made any response impossible. Strangers don't talk among themselves. What are they going to say? Since they are likely coming from different places and going to different ones also, what sense is there in a comment or a conversation? The chatter would break the equilibrium. They might say something pleasant, something disagreeable, something personal. It is for this reason that in spite of the quantity of people gathered there, there was a disproportionate silence, interrupted at times by warnings given through loudspeakers regarding the different flights, or by a suave and impersonal music that said nothing and represented nothing. A vague murmur was heard, as if a prayer were being recited by a chorus in low voices, but that was, fortunately, nothing more than the basic use of duly trained vocal chords. Heads, bodies, extremities (made in my own image and likeness) passed in contrary directions in front of the seat where I sat. Where they were going or where they had come from didn't interest me. The people passed, carried by the pure mechanics of their motion. They in turn ignored me, not from pride, vanity, or some cheap combination that so frequently produces poisonous and even irreparable wounds. Those hypocritical pretensions related to fondness, friendship, sympathy, affection (so stridently affected among *latino* peoples and no less evident in Anglo-Saxons), the whole pretended gamut of love (or of hate) that is expressed, disappeared in that community where (luckily) there was only indifference. The mutual ignorance in which we lived allowed for no love, but neither did it permit hate. What serene apathy! How absurd the feelings of humiliation and pride that we live through in circumstances dominated by rancor and personal envy. All those fantasies about the life we left behind, the attractiveness of our home town, family unity, the concept of friendship, the fidelity of our women, the masculinity of our men, the blue of our sky and the fine sand of Varadero, seemed stupid to me. Hadn't it all been a farce and was not that the only reality? I thought that I could pass my whole life (a hundred lives) in that waiting room in which I wasn't waiting for anything, in which no one waited for me or said goodbye, in which I knew no one (I had completely lost my notion of Amanda) and no one knew me, in which no one had time to note my presence

27

in the same way that I had no time to identify with anyone. Never in my life had I felt such an intense and authentic contact with my surroundings.

Soon something else caught my attention: the baggage. Many passengers went by with baggage, or porters carried their suitcases to the lines from which baggage was being dispatched. The baggage was varied and revealed multiple destinations, not only with respect to where it had come from, but to where it was going. The vastness of the building had carried me to such a state of psychic intensity that at first I didn't notice such important details. But soon the suitcases began exercising an attraction so strong I was shaken in the deepest way. If the people didn't awaken the least emotion in me, the possibilities of the baggage they carried began to stir hidden impulses. Because inside each suitcase there were enough items of an intimate nature to form a universe. They opened in my imagination like a kind of uterus from which creatures emerged disguised as things. Each bag was of the female sex, whose lips opened in a kiss so that I might penetrate them. There were strong sexual overtones among intimate articles that were transformed into vivid, tactile symbols or erotic evocations. For an instant I believed I was going crazy and thought that any moment I would throw myself like one possessed on top of the suitcases and experience a desperate orgasm. So overcome was I by these hallucinatory feelings and impulses that without wishing to I squeezed Amanda's hand to prove she was really there, alive at my side, but possibly because of the emotions I was experiencing at that moment I didn't dare look at her.

I tried to infuse my thoughts with more practical matters and get away from the erotic imagery. It was not easy. Until a sequence that was nakedly grotesque and painful interrupted the others; a suitcase with metal edges sharpened like knives was closed in the moment of copulation

and castrated me with its guillotine edges. After the frightening grief produced by this amputation, I was sunk in
an intense calm, faced as I was by the eradication of my
sex.

From then on, the suitcases acquired a more practical
aspect. What would happen if I made off, accidentally on
purpose, with some of those suitcases, pretending some
carelessness or confusion? Wouldn't some miraculous
transformation take place if we took one of them in place
of carrying ours, which didn't contain a thing of real
value? Because the articles that we had with us in our
suitcase (how much I despised myself when I thought of
that luggage! How cheap our existence was! And the
others who carried not just one but dozens of suitcases
full of all sorts of things, including even collapsing fur-
niture of the type that folds and folds and then unfolds
and unfolds until it becomes a summer camping tent, and
including even prefabricated buildings!) weren't worth
anything and we had nothing to lose in the exchange.
Needless to say that in the long run I didn't dare do any
of this and we had to resign ourselves to the misery of
our baggage. Besides, I was sure that Amanda wouldn't
approve the switch, perhaps because of some doodad of
a personal character (odds and ends to which Amanda
gave particular importance: a letter, a broken brooch, a
Christmas postcard that she had salvaged from the waste
basket) that she had managed to stick in our baggage.
Even though she found an authentic diamond in the suitcase, she would be lamenting the loss of some miserable
trifle for a long time. On the other hand, what guarantee
had we that what we found in the other suitcase would
serve us personally in any way? Some people carry useless,
absurd mementoes from places they visit, trinkets that
serve to pay back doubtful social debts. Other passengers
were much fatter or thinner than we were, and therefore

we were sure that their clothing wouldn't fit us well. Nevertheless, we would spot someone of my weight and stature, or with measurements similar to Amanda's, and speculate that in this way it would be possible to come on some good clothing of satisfactory fit. But it was obvious that if it was well within the realm of possibility to find someone whose measurements matched one of ours, it would be rather unlikely to find a couple whose measurements matched both. Besides, there existed some really extravagant people, persons who carried peculiar hobbies with them wherever they went, fearful perhaps that these articles would be stolen if they left them in their attractive empty houses. What would we do if we found ourselves with a suitcase full of bird feathers, a collection of rocks, heads captured in the Amazon jungles, dried lizards, buttons of every form and color or the teeth of widely varied animals? Anything was possible, and I was sure that if the venture failed Amanda would never forgive me.

These thoughts were interrupted finally when the moment came for the plane to leave. Because of bad weather the flight was most disagreeable. But in general there were no worse problems. We arrived in the North in full winter, and it was getting ready to snow by way of welcome. These conditions made it necessary, on getting off the airplane, to put on the overcoats in order to cross a runway that was half frozen. In the midst of the more immediate concerns and emotions of the trip, we didn't have time to think about the danger posed by those overcoats which a couple of nights ago had given rise to the unpleasant but undeniable incident that I have described. Now that we really had something to do, we were no longer conscious of the insignificant details that had caused us such alarm. But we realized one thing: the overcoats fulfilled the function for which they had been created. They protected us from the cold.

They did it better because the fit was large. We were reminded of this in the most unlooked-for way. On entering the building after crossing the runway on which we slipped and almost fell a couple of times, nearly breaking a leg, we were directed toward the place where we were supposed to collect our baggage. It was then, when, turning down a wide hallway, we encountered an immense mirror that gave us back our own images. For a moment we didn't recognize them. In the first place very little of our real selves remained visible. Amanda wore some black boots that came to her knees, and since the overcoat descended to her ankles her legs were completely covered, which is to say, well protected—most well protected!—against the bad weather. As her body and limbs were so perfectly hidden under the deformity of wool and skin that covered them, it occurred to me that the legs of "that woman" must be made of wood. The body of the coat was a very poorly cut black rectangle, and since she was wearing a black cloche that covered her ears, all that remained was the much reduced oval of her face. Amanda's face was so small that it was almost lost in her apparel, consumed even more by her tortoise-shell glasses that did not become her in any way. A little more and she wouldn't need a face and, what is worse, she wouldn't even be there.

In regards to "that man" (whom it is supposed was I), the appearance was no less grotesque. I had also clapped a hat on my head, a bit large, for it hid half my forehead. The brim of the hat was particularly wide, and as it was somewhat tired it fell listlessly over my ears, which were largely hidden. My glasses formed wide black loops made of some plastic material; the lenses were darkly tinted (since I was particularly sensitive to solar light) and made me look like the typical blind man who sells lottery tickets on corners. In recent years, in spite of my relative youth, my face had lengthened—what with the scarcity of food from which we had suffered in our country and in part because of the insecurity and uncertainty in which we lived—and I had lost considerable weight. This slimness, not bad when one has money to let it be known that it's not the product of suffering or hunger, produced an extraordinarily negative impression. It was a face (from the nose on down) that was long and melancholy, ending in a jutting jaw, as if the person who carried it had suffered a prolonged sickness. Meanwhile the hat with the crestfallen brim gave me the aspect of an Argentinean tango singer dying of advanced tuberculosis. Since I had raised the collar of the overcoat (because of the wind on the airport runway), covering the little that remained of my face, I also resembled a Chicago gangster. Although I was not very tall, the large overcoat, moth-eaten and threadbare, lengthened my figure; I practically walked on the cuffs of my wide and antiquated trousers since my waist failed to hold them up. I also wore black rubber boots and black gloves. For that reason I could easily have been a scarecrow on whom they had placed a human head (or half a human head).

But if it's true that we had a certain difficulty in recognizing ourselves, we immediately recognized the overcoats. This reaction was mutual and surprising and, something even stranger, it attracted us, united us spiritually, at the same time that it amused us. It lit up our faces and the mirror returned the smiles of those strange beings who were ourselves. Encouraged by that expression which gave new life to our confidence, we stopped and began to laugh in front of the mirror. The situation was, frankly, humorous and gaily Chaplinesque. Thank God that the laughter allowed us to recognize each other. All during the wait at the other airport we'd scarcely spoken, as if

in reality we were unknown travelers who by chance oc-
cupied the same bench. Now our presence in the mirror
reunited us again: we were images whose reflections recognized each other. And recognized each other more because of the coats than because of our faces. We turned
towards each other and realized that in effect we were
ourselves. One gloved hand united with another, reminding me of the small, delicate hand that Amanda had had.
    It took some effort to find a more or less decent place
to live. It wasn't surprising that people were suspicious
of us, considering our grotesque aspect. It wasn't that
their appearance was much better. Usually their looks
were so disagreeable that on a number of occasions we
were glad that they found something suspicious and unpleasant in us. What were we going to do if one of that
monstrous brotherhood that opened shabby doors to us
had bid us welcome and said he had a free room? The
categorical no that we received seemed at times like an
escape from the inferno. Everyone had an accent that in
no way resembled the language of the land. They pronounced their words as badly or worse than we did, which
caused our way of speech to become an accent within an
accent, creating a terrible distinction that put us in a situation even more invidious. Nothing ever went well. At
times it was I who spoke in the hope of having mastered
the accent of someone who had previously rejected me.
When the door half opened, a dirty suspicious face with
disheveled hair would show itself in the shadows, murmuring something which I never managed to understand.
"Have you a free room?" I asked, falsifying my voice and
trying to imitate that accent which was not correct in a
phonetic sense, but was correct to their ears, or what we
supposed was correct. Naturally we failed again and again.
They looked at us amazed and we had to repeat ourselves
in front of eyes which grew ever more astonished before

the two strange beings who didn't know the accent within the accent. At times they slammed the door in our faces, murmuring something in an accent that was normal for them but to our ears sounded like an insult. The kindest ones made us repeat the question various times, in all the accents, until finally they repeated it with their own: "Ah, do we have a free room!"—but we couldn't distinguish the difference between accents. Other times Amanda would speak with the greatest propriety, using the true accent (and she managed to do it correctly after various tries), but it always worsened our situation, as if that pronunciation were an insult, a personal affront, completely in disaccord, besides, with our appearance, since we had been obliged to insert the repugnant accent within the accent within the accent. After interminable wanderings our predicament finally came to an end when someone decided to overlook our appearance and our accent.

We rented a room with a little kitchen, but no bath, in a building on 14th St. The building was clean, but its general aspect was seedy. Nevertheless, our budget didn't permit anything better. Right away we decided to start looking for work and went to an employment agency. We had to wait for some time in a vestibule where there were approximately a dozen folding chairs lined up as if in penitence against the wall. But this time we didn't attract particular attention. Although some looked at us out of the corners of their eyes, not everyone did, and we realized (without mentioning it to each other) that a process of assimilation had begun to take place. Especially in Amanda's case. One woman a little older than the rest smiled at her and said something which, naturally, we didn't understand, but to which Amanda responded with an expressive smile and such brilliance in her eyes (like the brilliance of dogs who appear to understand human beings) that she gave unequivocal signs of understanding, although she apprehended nothing. Then Amanda made an unexpected gesture. She took off that frightening black cloche which hid half her face and ran a hand through her hair that, although flattened and disfigured by the weight of the hat, still retained the grace of some natural waves that returned to her a part of her lost and genuine elegance. A pair of old men looked at her with marked interest and a woman of approximately our age smiled skeptically (not at me, but at Amanda's gesture), as if it were all a farce. It was then they called us for the interview.

The man who attended us had a pleasing appearance and must have been tall, although it was hard to be sure, seated as he was behind a desk that was covered with papers in the greatest disorder (as if he had disarranged them on purpose and left them that way for some time). His distinguishing mark was his wavy white hair, which also shone intensely, but which was nevertheless not greasy or clinging. His hair revealed his age (some fifty years, which he carried lightly), but in spite of his shining appearance (or perhaps because of it) there was something obscene and libidinous about him. My presence immediately struck him as wrong, but he was subsequently impressed by Amanda, whose corporal existence he wanted to reach above (or below) the overcoat. It was evident that he was used to looking at people in this way, and it would not be the first time that a beautiful body (and I do not say it specifically of Amanda) would have hidden itself uselessly in a heavy sack of wool. His interest notwithstanding, it was clear that my presence did not warrant his scrutiny. He told us that at this time there was very little demand for unskilled labor, but although "naturally" there was absolutely nothing for me he could offer Amanda a job in a costume factory that was near the wharfs. Although we didn't understand the reasons for that "naturally," we were not in a position to argue about it, so Amanda accepted the offer immediately. The man added that although it was not the best thing for "a woman of her position," it was the only opening he had, and she must not hesitate to come back in the not very distant future, when he'd probably have something better to offer her. For me, he repeated, there was nothing, "naturally."

In spite of the interview, which had been unpleasant, Amanda was excited by the prospect of work, "particularly," she said, "in a costume factory." For me that datum ("in a costume factory") was no more significant than work, for example, in a watch factory. Amanda said it was completely different. She never would have accepted work in a watch factory, nor in one for mirrors. But a factory for disguises was full of significance and gave new life to her imagination. The idea, nevertheless, was disturbing. I didn't insist because I had not the least desire to upset her.

On getting off the subway at 14th St., the stop nearest our lair, we found the temperature had dropped considerably. It had begun to snow and the sidewalks were wet and dirty, which made it impossible to hurry. In order not to fall, I set down my feet heavily, causing the dirty slush to splash one way and the other, frequently spattering Amanda's boots. The people went forward trembling as if it were impossible ever to accustom themselves to such bad weather. For our part and in spite of the fact we were extremely sensitive to the cold, we felt relatively comfortable inside our overcoats. Although old, ugly, and threadbare, the overcoats fulfilled their function perfectly. Never again would we speak of that ridiculous incident, and in spite of my words to the contrary such a sensation of warmth, security, and confidence seemed to arise from them that the initial suspicion was replaced by blind faith;

above all in the case of Amanda, who had gained, because of the work, a greater self-confidence.

It is necessary to take into account that we were in an immense and desolate city situated to the north of our country, and under climatological conditions that were in reality pitiless. We were alone, we knew nobody. There were lots of people, but all completely indifferent to what was happening to us or might happen. Each seemed dizzily rushing to fulfill the particular circumstances of his own life, caught up in his own abandon, in his own overcoat. Nothing seemed to exist beyond those woolen borders (or skin in some cases) that seemed to adhere as they do to animals (the dog, the rabbit, the cat, the mouse, the squirrel; and so many others it would make the list interminable) that don't need overcoats because they seem to carry them already, were born with them. This practical sense in animals is surprising and it's natural that we (man) should imitate it, trying to attach ourselves to the overcoat that protects us so effectively from the out-of-doors. This explains, perhaps, the preference of men (and women in particular) for overcoats of skin (which are the most expensive), where the animal sense increases as if we had succeeded in acquiring the skin of a rabbit, a mink, a leopard, a tiger, an antelope, in order to have a more natural heat, a second and more authentic one which is more animal. Don't those hairy overcoats offer a special sensation of protection just to look at them? In our poverty we felt pleased by that heat which the overcoats offered us, the only generous thing we could count on in that moment. Everything else was cold, indifferent. But the overcoats had the unselfish generosity, the familiar warmth, that friendly intimacy that we met nowhere else. They provided in that moment the only love our bodies received.

On arriving at the apartment we felt that it was like a freezer. It was not the first time, however. Ever since we rented it, Amanda had said that it resembled an ice chest, but since it was relatively clean and it was a little less unpleasant than the others we had seen, and since they made no conditions, we had decided to rent it and ignore the cold. The room obviously rejected us. Doesn't one react in a similar way in front of persons who treat us with marked chilliness? The apartment didn't try to hide the little sympathy it felt for us, assuming we could measure its attitude by its "coldness." The first night I decided to go down and complain to the manager, especially since Amanda insisted on it. While going down the stairs, I again had one of those ridiculous thoughts to which I was lately becoming prey. All at once my complaint seemed like tittle-tattle. Was it right that I should criticize that apartment and tell an unknown that it was "very cold"? If we were strangers to it, what reason had we to demand more heat? Because we were paying? Perhaps, because prostitutes ought to feign warmth even though they're frigid. It is for this that we pay them. In any case, I was irritated, as if embarked on a fool's errand, irked that I should be the one to complain that it was not "hot" and the manager had failed in doing his duty. Evidently put out, he looked at me as if I were some repugnant gossip monger and told me there was nothing he could do because the heater was set at its maximum and it was sufficiently "warm." Quick as a wink, he slammed the door in my face. The blanket which covered the bed was, according to Amanda, "as thin as a sheet," incapable of protecting us against the intense cold that existed in that room, and we were in no condition to buy blankets for the winter. Therefore, we had to do the best we could with what we had in reach; in other words, the overcoats. Beginning with the first night, we decided not to take them off for fear of pneumonia, and from then on our lives were passed in our overcoats. This custom began to create an unpleasant estrangement between us. On going to bed, we exchanged a furtive kiss, sometimes an embrace, but it ended in that contact of black wool that appeared to have replaced our skins. The sensation produced was one of intimate repulsion, but we were too tired, oppressed, and nearly frozen to do other than we did.

Under such conditions Amanda began her job as manual laborer. I accompanied her to the subway entrance and saw her disappear in the midst of a multitude that every moment looked more the same. When she went off, it was as if "everyone went." This idea occurred to me confusedly, but it was clarified when, at the subway entrance, I began watching the other women, without doubt day laborers, who entered in interminable succession. It was certainly true they all didn't look like Amanda, although the majority did. Others, more in the mode, "dressed like secretaries," and in the midst of that cold left open to view some slender and well-formed legs.

In the beginning, during those first weeks, as soon as I separated from Amanda I began my tour of employment agencies. The first few days I tried to cover an unrealistically high number and quickly reached the limit of my strength. The distances were impossible and frequently I got lost, walking block after block in a direction opposite to the one I was trying to go. All of them looked the same, and there was even an occasion when I became so mixed up that I went twice to the same agency, wasting time in the most miserable way and not realizing the mistake until I had spent a good time waiting. The procedure of the agencies was more or less the same, and the announcements were made in an impersonal, staccato tone that made it impossible to tell one from another. The street and room numbers were the only distinguishing features, and since I never was very good at mathematics the errors were sufficiently frequent. In any case, it didn't matter. The result was always the same, and I might just as well have gone to the same one every day since the outcome was always negative. Although I wasn't completely out of step with the others who sought work, there was something about me that produced rejection the moment I appeared before the employee who made the lists and gave the interviews. He might not say "naturally," but he did insist that "there are no vacancies for unskilled workers." Amanda encouraged me, said not to give up hope, that everyone at the factory was saying it was a bad moment to get work and that at least we wouldn't starve to death, because she had something. Without doubt, they thought "someone" had helped her. It followed naturally and absolutely that I would find nothing. But others somehow, I thought, found work because I saw them leave (many of them) with the little white card that was the sure sign they had found something. Then, out of curiosity, I found myself watching them during my long and frequent waits. It's possible I might have lost track of myself, stuffed as I was into someone else's overcoat. Since I passed my life in that old overcoat which didn't even belong to me, I was losing a clear image of my own person. But little by little I was beginning to see that although others looked much as I did, there were many whose condition was more presentable, sometimes because of some detail in their dress (shinier shoes, a gay and stylish tie, a ring with some odd stone that attracted attention) or because of a more positive attitude, including a false smile. In me there was nothing positive, nor a manner which suggested it, except that I sat in those chairs that helped augment the monotony of waiting, with the full consciousness that failure was not going to separate me from that worn and moth-eaten woolen overcoat.

For this reason I stopped trying so hard and decided to go to only one agency a day. I began to feel an extraordinary fear that I would use them all up and then I would find myself in a situation even more desperate, for I'd have nowhere to go during the day. It was another of those absurd ideas that occurred to me with increasing frequency, since with employment agencies filling pages and pages in the telephone book it would be years before I could visit all of them. Perhaps I should set such thoroughness as a goal and then my life would take on a new meaning. I didn't believe it possible that someone might appear and tell me, yes, they did have work for unskilled personnel. Since I was visiting only one agency and didn't know how to fill my days unless I continued making these futile gestures, I preferred to go to the most distant and used the better part of the morning getting there. No matter how quickly they took care of me (something that did not generally occur), I always had the entire afternoon to return. Fortunately the waits were long and little by little I became accustomed to them, preferring a long wait to a short one, for it gave me time to rest up from those interminable excursions while at the same time warming up. Many times I slept a little, and since I was usually congealed on account of those constant comings and goings along inhospitable sidewalks, and as the cold seemed to have penetrated my bones, I never took off the overcoat in spite of the fact that after a couple of hours had passed I was invaded by a species of asphyxia that did not quite seem real. The central heating, the foul air, the hermetically sealed windows, produced in me a kind of suffocating torpor that nevertheless seemed pleasant.

One day I had a terrible experience. In spite of the delicate nature of the matter, I am faced with the painful

41

necessity of having to relate it since it is necessary that everything here must have the stamp of truth. I had been walking about three hours in search of a rather distant employment agency. Since in reality the agency was far away, I didn't have to pretend that I was lost (one of my more frequent tricks, although I hated to do it), and the trek was indeed difficult. Because of the cold I felt the necessity to urinate. This need occurred frequently, but it was more intense on the coldest days; the same is true with everybody, I believe. The compulsion was purely mechanical and I tried to find a urinal. I entered a cafeteria of the popular type (one of those known as "automatics," in which the service is completely impersonal, at times by means of little windows where there is a plate behind glass and you deposit the money in a slot and the little window opens and you seize the dish) and searched out the sign leading to the restroom. I recognized, in short, the perfunctory nature of the matter and soon found myself standing before a urinal. On opening the overcoat quickly and beginning to urinate, I felt an inexplicable horror take hold of me as I felt that flaccid organ that was hanging from my body. The act is so routine that frequently one does it unconsciously, but in that moment I was absolutely conscious of what I was doing, as if it were one of the most transcendent deeds of my entire life. The sensation in the tips of my fingers as they contacted that flesh was so wounding and so empty that I felt myself transfixed by a unique anguish and knew that if I looked the sensation would be even sharper because sight would be added to the bother (I'm not sure that's the right word) that touch produced. I did it, nevertheless, and saw that thing my hand sustained and that presented itself to my eyes as an appendage of meat. It appeared to me as an absolutely impersonal organ with no identifying characteristics, much more undefined than the hand which sustained

42

it mechanically or than the eyes which viewed it. But the worst part took place when it occurred to me I hadn't the least certainty that organ was mine and not someone else's, although it hung exactly where mine should have been. What certainty was there that we were one and the same? And if another urinated through this conduit and not myself? And if that urine that emerged was not mine but the urine of some other creature, a strange creature that inhabited me? I finished urinating and made haste to place that organ inside the overcoat and got out of there in a state of horror almost. It was necessary that I face up to the situation in which I found myself and that meant a careful investigation. The only solution was that I undress, that I examine my body to make sure that everything belonged and that that dangling appendage and all the organs that went with it were mine. I remembered the adage—"you can shake them, but they won't fall off"— and to the worry of what I had "felt" and "seen" was added the terrible expectancy that not only might it not be mine, but that the gross popular saying was not quite right and there existed the remote possibility (not so remote) that it would jiggle and fall. I had to return to the apartment as soon as possible and perform a visual and tactile inspection of my body in order to regain full confidence in my being—it wasn't just the organs of my body, but the body itself. Didn't the inverse possibility also exist, that I had no existence except in that? But at the same time that I made the decision to return to the apartment and all during the time I was going back, I didn't even dare to touch those organs through my clothing. I was afraid. It was for this reason that the closer I drew to our cave, the more I felt an impulse to retrace my steps coming over me, a suspicion I was losing my mind and that I ought to return to the employment agency because this might well be the day they had work. I knew that the argument was a trick to fool myself, that I was playing games with myself so I wouldn't discover anything. But I insisted on telling myself that it was unjust for Amanda to be working in the factory when I wasn't dedicating all my time to seeking employment, allowing myself to be carried away by childish thoughts. These arguments were gaining in strength, and I decided to retrace my steps since I was covering blocks in the wrong direction. Nevertheless, on arriving at one of the entrances to the subway, I had the most violent, unrestrainable impulse and ducked into that dark cavity (something I never did because I was trying to save my last penny) and took an underground train that would carry me in the shortest possible time to the stop at 14th St., which was the nearest to the building where we lived. On the train I felt calmer and I told myself several times that all I had to do was strip myself to prove once and for all that my body was whole. I left the station relatively calm and disposed to undress. I arrived at our building, climbed the stairs, opened the door of our room and closed it after me, running the deadbolt. Then I found myself confronted with that possibility, or those possibilities: the physical integrity of my being or the infinite possibilities of its pieces. But the dangers of knowing were too great, and as the reader will have imagined I did nothing. I allowed myself to fall on the bed, overcoat and all.

When Amanda arrived she wasn't able to open the door, and she asked me why I had locked it from inside.

CHAPTER

3

On a morning when the sun was making one of its rare efforts to break the monotony of winter, I walked toward a gray park, its trees without leaves. It had a run-down look. After that last strange disturbance I had remained strangely empty, as if my soul wandered in the gray atmosphere that seemed an extension of the asphalt of the streets, of the concrete of the buildings, of the dirty current of the river, up to and including the monotony of a sky in which the blue seemed to have disappeared forever. I wasn't thinking anything in particular. Instead my thoughts were diffuse, distracted to the point where I wasn't aware of my natural surroundings. The condition seemed healthful to me because thoughts of a different character could produce a dangerous disequalibrium. I had, nevertheless, the remote notion of a sun that struggled to produce light, and a new peacefulness began to come over me. I realized it was absolutely useless to walk so far looking for an agency at which I pretended to find work. Ultimately I had reached the extreme of giving contradictory answers when I filled out the application blanks, with the sole intention of making myself even more suspicious and avoiding at all costs the chance of being offered work—this last, certainly, very unlikely but not impossible. It followed, perhaps, that there were other means of distraction and amusement without my having to cover half the city in search of such adventures. The presence of the park, not far from where we lived, made me consider such a possibility. Besides, I was really growing more tired each day. As I had no appetite, I hardly ate, which was also a boon to the pocketbook—an aspect of our lives in which Amanda took intense interest. But it was evident that each day I had less energy and that any sort of effort was burdensome. Consequently the gray park with that interminable succession of gray benches that lost themselves in the distance, under gray trees or trunks that were almost black (like the masterpiece of a blind painter who has lost all sense of color), came to dominate my weariness.

I sat down on one of those benches, looked at my surroundings and began to understand the reasons behind some of the things that had been happening to me lately. Not all, however. A toothless old man with eyes that seemed to lose themselves in the depths of their sockets, like remote inaccessible planets in unknown outer space, looked at me with a malicious smile, his mouth compressed in an extended grin that never broke and that arose as much from those round gray planets in those remote sockets as it did from his lips. The smile had something of the fascination and insulting ambiguity of a Mona Lisa. Here it must be said that it had nothing to do with the eternal feminine or masculine—as might possibly occur with the famous smile that has a sex only by accident. Because it was one of those enigmas beyond sexuality, whose answer is never reached. I remembered that disquieting image (of Mona Lisa), so homely, so contrary (that no one understands and that makes us feel such discomfort, as if she—the smile—knew something that we

46

didn't); that she was always reminding us of our stupidity in the face of her understanding—although possibly she knows no more than we do, but pretends she does and since you can't prove she doesn't, it's absolutely useless to try to deny it. In any case, it is an influence we can't escape because her eyes or her mouth pursue us like a "big brother is watching you," refusing to leave us in peace, in sunlight or in shadow. These ideas passed through my head on confronting those little eyes which were not going to leave me for a long time.

The face was familiar to me in spite of the fact I was sure I had never seen it before. But what struck me as really familiar (more than the face) was the aspect: the hat that covered half the forehead, the brim which fell listlessly over the ears, the collar turned up to offer greater protection against the cold and the wind, the overcoat which fell like a large flabby sarcophagus. He looked at me fixedly, the little eyes always revolving in the depths of their universe, like a double constellation of stars, mocking and lightly affable, expressive and titillating. They created the contradictory sensations of the surprise one experiences on meeting an old friend that he really doesn't know. I wanted to escape, but it was obvious I was not going to be able to do it because the riddle of that toothless smile and those eyes that smiled at me from the depths of a cavern, or a night, offered such a hidden fascination that you felt you were never going to be able to separate yourself from them until you discovered their significance, although you also knew that such discovery was never going to take place. We would remain on the bench and pass hours and hours there, looking fixedly one at the other.

The reader should not believe that this had to do with a fantastic apparition. In no way. I must insist that everything I tell took place within the borders of normality.

47

Nothing is unreal. If the reader has at some time been in one of those northern cities, like London or New York, with their large parks of perfect grass, or in their other parks which are not so large or perfect—dirty and abandoned rather, with bottles of gin thrown here and there and the drunks not very far, some on the grass, others more discreetly on benches—he will realize that I am not talking about a fantastic apparition. On the contrary. That such a man should be here was the most natural thing in the world.

Then I understood what was happening to me, and even that quiet "naturally" of the dirty old man at the employment agency. The overcoat so identified me with a certain group that I could not free myself from the circumstances to which all its members were condemned. How was it possible that a responsible agent of the community was going to offer work, even as an unskilled laborer, to someone with all the marks of a bonafide vagabond? The practical reasons for what was happening to me (that is to say, my unemployment) were quite logical. The situation was clear and there was no other interpretation, nor was one necessary.

Where, then, could I turn? What could I do except sit on that desolate bench and stare, allowing myself to be looked at for hours and hours by those puzzling little eyes where everything was explained but nothing was solved? The consciousness of my absolute expulsion from the outer world (and I call the outer world everything outside of me, including Amanda) was more present than ever. And although the smile repulsed me, at least that face fixed on my face, those penetrating little eyes, that buried chin which fit the mouth without teeth, that smile which was something between malevolent and familiar, and especially that old overcoat—ten times older and more threadbare than mine, but which was, simply, a worn-out replica of the one I had on—produced a feeling of intimacy in me in the face of rejection, of confidence within my gloomy imaginings, of warmth in a winter that was beyond any of the inclemencies I had ever lived through; it was, in short, my only recourse.

Was that my companionship? If so, it was rather doubtful company, but it commanded my full faith that it was the only thing possible in my situation. I couldn't ascertain what company was possible in Amanda's—that woman who was so active and met life from such a different position. The truth was that already Amanda provided me not with company, but solitude, and my estrangement from her (precisely because of the overcoat) appeared without remedy. Being uprooted historically and geographically had produced in us a total estrangement— after which, ironically, my heart beat with the need for company. What was this company? Evidently I was not it for Amanda, nor Amanda for me. Why? The logical reasons escaped me and the guilt lay in the overcoat—"In the overcoats, you mean," Amanda might have replied to me had I asked her. But in that wintry park the overcoats acquired a completely different significance (my overcoat, I mean), and it appeared that I was going to find there, on those benches where my overcoat didn't clash, but was exactly in the mode; that I was going to find, I say, companionship.

For a long time we never spoke. I believe we hadn't spoken. I think that days passed and we never said a word; years, centuries. I don't remember exactly. I looked at him and he looked at me, the two of us, as if staring into a void. What did he see in me? Did my eyes revolve there behind my glasses, within the two remote sockets completely removed, like planets you can never reach, separated from the rest of the universe by thousands of light years? Was I and not he the riddle of the picture? Did I also belong in the same indecipherable category and was it for this reason that the Mona Lisa never took her eyes from me, not mocking me, but eternally mocking herself? The contact of our eyes in space produced an interminable chain of possibilities. The idea was enriched by mystery, and the impossibility of a reply was what permitted an eternity of questions. Questions? Were we really asking each other something? Because I, in reality, couldn't sustain a single question. It was almost a look for a look— the brutal history of an eye for an eye.

These things notwithstanding, I must not ignore the socio-economic side of these events, since in a sense everything began because of my isolation inside the overcoat. Meeting someone similar immediately produced a class identification. I wish to take advantage of this moment to point out that given my atypical temperament it was impossible for me to identify with those who, like I, had abandoned the island and who got together to drink coffee (or at times beer), mixed with milk and swear words, make indecent jokes and cast lecherous glances at the backsides of women who passed near them, as if they were going to eat them with their eyes—their backsides, I mean. Their speech put me off and I was driven by temperament to go in search of other frontiers.

It was providential, therefore, to discover the park, where nationality was not at issue and which was therefore more in keeping with my gloomy state of mind. Other men, all older than I and dressed in a similar fashion, were scattered throughout the park, seated two and two, or in larger groups perhaps. There were some, nevertheless, who remained alone, their heads downcast as if asleep, their faces completely hidden (as if they had none) under the fallen brims of their hats. Here and there one or another slept heavily—who knew if drunk—occupying a bench at full length. Some dirty-looking doves pecked at the cement. It was no mistake that there was not one completely white dove among them.

An observer who was not prejudiced might have been surprised at the peaceful atmosphere in that park. It seemed like a peaceful club of aristocrats or monied persons, possibly Londoners, in which men over fifty, merchants, retired industrialists, honorable politicians, let the hours pass with a glass of their favorite drink in hand, and before their eyes, impassible as Henry James's, the *London Times*. The scene wasn't so distant from that reality, since old newspapers rested peacefully on legs covered by ragged wool.

That first day went by in the most absolute calm, uninterrupted, I think, by a single word. Possibly there was a moment when we were on the point of saying something, but as luck would have it I couldn't find a single word, or so it seemed. We would look at each other as if confronting the riddle of the Sphinx, although it didn't seem to me I had a trace of that astuteness, unlike him, who affected it as if in reality he were on the right track. From a distance others observed us, as if recognizing someone recently arrived. No one appeared to speak much, but there was no lack of looks in my direction, coming from the group as a whole. I soon decided that instead of being equal I was different, although the observation was tempered by the fact that all of us had a similar appearance. From time to time, as the day drew on, someone would get up and pass slowly in front of the bench where my friend and I were sitting, looking at us from the corner of his eye as he went by. At times he would come back, doing the same thing from the opposite direction. Another old man who looked very much like the one sitting beside me, but with a marked hump that distinguished him from the rest, went by many times, looking at me even more fixedly, turning his head slightly and making a kind of nod (almost imperceptible) that had something of the Chinese about it. For a moment I thought he was going to say something, but he never managed to do it. The more discreet ones, as I have already indicated, watched furtively from afar as if I were a new and unlooked-for spectacle.

Since the cold was really intolerable and it was getting dark, I got up. The old man looked at me and, very timidly, stretched out his hand to touch the sleeve of my overcoat. It was a touch so delicate that I didn't feel it, saw it only, although I should have felt it through the moth-eaten wool of the overcoat. It was, without doubt, a friendly invitation to return. I didn't dare to answer, not because I doubted it (since I was going to return), but because I was afraid of expressing the absolute security a response would have implied. To return was for me inevitable and I don't know quite what would have happened to me in that moment if someone had opposed these intentions. I was, at any rate, slightly discourteous. Some old men saw me go by and others got up (as if the spectacle were over) and went off in a direction contrary to the one I was going.

I had made myself late and had to hurry. I was always in the apartment before Amanda arrived and wanted to hide (particularly) my activities of that day. I couldn't explain why, but I was sure that Amanda ought not to know about them. I didn't want to raise suspicions. But, of what exactly would those suspicions consist? I didn't have the least idea, but I understood that it had to do with a world which Amanda was forbidden from entering.

Besides, Amanda appeared halfway happy. She had accepted her new job valorously and was confronting the adversities of life with a courage that should have won her, at the very least, a medal. With regard to me it was fair to say, when all was said and done, that what was happening wasn't my fault. Amanda herself had considered that hobo overcoat the most appropriate piece of apparel. Now we would have to suffer the consequences; although I, in that moment, began to be glad of the choice. There wasn't the least doubt that Amanda's overcoat, from a practical point of view, had been a much happier choice.

When Amanda arrived, I was already in the apartment. The room still had what Amanda was used to calling, rather poetically, "inner cold"; and it was true one became congealed here as much, or more, than in the street. While she was preparing something to eat, there was a relative warmth in the apartment, but with each passing day our meals were becoming more infrequent. Amanda had decided that the best she could do was "to make lunch" (she was beginning to use those doubtful Anglicisms fairly frequently) and that I could do as well in a fast food outlet. After all, since I had lost my appetite and the meal frequently stuck in my throat, it wasn't worth her effort to cook anything, especially in that miserable oven where cooking was a hellish experience. For these reasons we usually settled in the evenings for some slices of ham, baloney, large sausage or some such thing and, to warm ourselves up, perhaps some coffee with milk. To me everything seemed fine and I was not about to ask Amanda for greater efforts. She was doing enough. Besides, the only thing you really wanted was to go to bed, to forget that miserable existence in the cramped apartment, to wrap yourself as tightly as possible in your respective overcoat and throw yourself on the bed to bury the memory of the day just past and the one that lay ahead. It was the only way to feel yourself halfway—no, no, by the furthest stretch—comfortable.

It's fair to say that we couldn't blame the overcoats for our estrangement. To do so would be too easy. Perhaps we would have to throw the blame on the apartment, which because of its frozen state obliged us to remain in

53

our overcoats—although we well might have found heat in the mutual sharing of our bodies. At all events, the overcoats saved us from a certain death by freezing. It was so agreeable to survive within them! It was as if one existed inside something, as if a cave protected and sheltered us, perhaps lulled us maternally. I vaguely remembered my first Freudian lectures during adolescence and told myself that it was a return to the womb. What tranquility! What total security! Sometimes I imagined cradle songs that the overcoat sang to me and a mild seasickness came over me, as if the overcoat rocked me in its arms. Other times the sensation was cosmic, and sometimes in bed I covered my head with it and felt myself travel through starry, nocturnal spaces. How far from me was Amanda in those moments! She floated toward other galaxies, enveloped in her black overcoat within which her head was not visible. Still other times the overcoat bathed me in a suffocating, sexual warmth. The silk lining had the slippery smoothness of damp skin and its contact produced the dizziness and ecstacy of an orgy.

When morning came (as if it were an extension of the night), there was no time for unnecessary confidences. Amanda had to hurry, for if she was late to work they took it out of her wages. At first I wanted to share some of my nocturnal experiences with her, but the exigencies of life interposed themselves and estrangement became a habit. I always thought that when night came we could talk, but when night came Amanda returned too tired to sustain a conversation or even to keep her eyes open for a prolonged period. I, for my part, felt generally depressed, without the spirit to insist on personal accounts that might lead us nowhere. Silence was the most effective coin.

In reality, I think all this took place before the encounter in the park, but it's necessary to make reference to it before getting into what the park meant to me. The park came along to increase the abyss that separated us.

At first (I repeat) when I was uneasy and felt depressed by not finding work, Amanda showed evident concern for my circumstances. Later, the failure of not finding it began to be a routine, and she seemed to notice that I had entered into a kind of indolence where the failure hardly mattered. She left off asking questions, and if she inquired at all it was only to be polite, as if she really expected no reply on my part. During the day nothing was said of the matter, and she ceased trying to determine what agency I had gone to or stopped going to, or what efforts I had made or had ceased making. It was tacitly assumed that having done something (was it that she had begun to doubt it?), whatever it was led to nothing other than failure.

I must not be unjust to Amanda during that period of our married life. Why should I reproach her for knowing so little of what was happening to me when I knew little more of her life? Could I claim to take an interest in her and say what she was experiencing day after day? It was evident that we moved on two different planes and that the sharing of our nightly lair was nothing more than an accidental circumstance. She turned suddenly enthusiastic over things which to me appeared to have come from another planet and that nevertheless were logical, absolutely normal. For example, one day she came home very excited because the season of greatest demand had arrived—although I, "naturally," could not find work anywhere. That meant that production had to increase and that the workers were obliged to exert themselves to the maximum. Overtime work brought double pay. She would also be able to work Saturdays because the orders for costumes had increased in a way that was simply extraordinary and the factory had too much to do, a circumstance which I personally didn't understand—how it was possible for demand to increase for a product that bore no relation to reality. For my part, I had no interest in discussing the matter, and of course I made no response whatever to Amanda. The ultimate causes that determined a work speed-up were beyond her scope. The only aspect that interested her (with much common sense) was immediate gain. Did she think perhaps that this increased activity was going to widen the distance that separated us? Did she think about that distance? Apparently not, but it would be a mistake to say I really knew what it was she thought. Her life appeared bound by a simple routine, tiring, yes, but without complications, in which doing piecework was both her immediate and ultimate objective. But that very acceptance of life by a temperament that had always been fundamentally rebellious was, in truth, profoundly suspect. Something strange was occurring inside of her also. Something that she wasn't telling me, that she wasn't communicating, that she was hiding jealously from me. What was happening in that body that could possibly be controlled by her overcoat? I had moments (when will power was highest) in which I might have wished to penetrate the prohibited world underneath that lustrous black wool. Because if I had my world, she undoubtedly had hers. But with that absurd attitude so common in human beings, we both pretended the most absolute indifference, as if we lived outside it all and nothing was happening.

How could it be that Amanda, who had always been conscious of my least movements, should show such a marked lack of interest in what was taking place inside my overcoat? And why had I made no decision to ask her openly about what was happening inside hers? Why was I impelled to maintain that distance that perhaps would cease to exist with a few words of clarification? But what words should I say in order for recognition to take place?

The truth is that the overcoats had involved us in a vicious circle marked by isolation. As I never touched her and since her most visible feature was her head, I often thought she was one of those old-fashioned dolls which have fragile porcelain heads sewn to bodies filled with sawdust. And if that was she, what was holding me together, a scarecrow with a broad-brimmed hat and open arms, crucified and planted in the middle of a field? When I saw her drawn away by the dark underground cavity that took her from me and carried her toward the bowels of the subway, I had the absolute certainty that her legs were made of wood. It calmed me to think that she might easily believe the same of my body and that nevertheless my old body was there, the same as always, under the external reality of the overcoat. Was? Then I agonized over my conflicting thoughts: and if one day she came to think that it wasn't thus, that I didn't exist? That would be the absolute proof that she didn't either.

This consciousness of loneliness was really intolerable, and had it not been for the park I think I would have inevitably turned to suicide.

The park, in short, signaled a complete change of life-style.

I had completely given up searching for work and every morning, as soon as I left Amanda, had seen her go off toward her subterranean connection, I hurried toward the park. How slow were the moments leading up to that separation! We didn't have (Amanda and I) anything to say to each other because my mind wandered in a realm which she didn't share and which was an enigma even to me. She was more active than ever, as if the significance of her existence depended on a production schedule. Little by little she began to wax enthusiastic over the number of masks that passed through her hands and how she had learned the difficult task of sewing on the plastic hairs that some of the masks featured. Nothing that she said to me held the least interest, and I saw her committed to a routine that was absolutely foreign to me.

When I arrived at the park, my friend was always there. At first I sat on a bench somewhat removed and solitary and he would come over later, timidly, with his accustomed smile, and sit on a bench a little apart from mine. As I have already indicated, I don't know how long we went without speaking. The time passed slowly and it didn't matter because we had nothing to do except preside over its passage. It swept over us and we remained immobile, feeling that caress of the hours that was something like a breeze. There were no desires, no anxieties, nothing. Other vagrants came later and observed us from a distance, respectfully, without hurrying either, as if it was part of a secret ceremony, a religious act, a mass performed in time under the gray vault of the sky.

Since we weren't speaking, I began to observe his overcoat in detail. The fellow had an overcoat identical to mine, but more opulent, attractive, old-fashioned. It had the weight of centuries. I came to look at it with astonished, devoted eyes as though it were a holy relic. For me it had the richness of one of those chasubles bordered in gold, medieval, that are exhibited in the showcases of sacristies, with a hundred arabesques that one can follow at a glance almost to eternity. It was totally unlike the insipid, colorless overcoats that were seen in the store windows, new, chilly, and lifeless as the manikins who wore them. That dirty worn-out overcoat appeared full of history, not through the impersonal hands of those who had made it, nor through the machines, but by the signs of miserable daily existence that seemed to have accumulated on each millimeter of cloth. The presence of that overcoat awoke infinite desires in me to emulate it. It wasn't that I wished to have his, but that mine might some day be that which his was now. It would be then, like his, the jewel of an antiquarian, consecrated by a cult of the ages.

Since his was a Prussian blue, I wasn't immediately aware of the wealth of shades it offered. Little by little I subjected it to my scrutiny, even taking off the dark glasses I nearly always wore, in order to see it better. I began to observe the ill-defined spots made by some unknown substance that appeared to be bordered, at intervals, by little silver threads. The overcoat was covered with stains, the residue of old meals that had accumulated one on top of the other until they formed the most subtle designs, almost imperceptible lines between one color and the other. I couldn't say exactly what each spot consisted of, where one ended and another began, or if, in reality, some part of the overcoat was free of spots and presented the original color in all its purity (although a faded purity), or at least some piece of its initial blue that was not covered by a thick scab of some dirty substance. Because it was not simply the uncleanliness of accumulated dust. That would have been unimportant. It was a dense filth: grease, soup, juice, alcohol, vomit, excrement, snot. Of course, these things were not in a certain sense there (which might have been repulsive), but the very essence of all that, as if the substances that constituted the organized and systematic putrefaction of the body had worked virulently toward the surface, where they manifested themselves as an esthetic abstraction. The uncleanliness, acting as artist, had projected the designs of its own rot on the wool. Just as children follow the movement of clouds, following their changes in order to discover monsters, I passed whole hours trying to decipher the historic plenty of that petrified corruption.

But it was difficult. There was an air of mystery, as if it had something to do with a romantic tale where diffuse images appeared superimposed one on the other. My imagination supplied, then, what the pure truth left out. What did that greenish line with a certain luster represent, that began over one of the lapels of the overcoat and extended a little below until it disappeared in the blue? Perhaps it was the historic condensation of a vomit which the air had dried and purified until it changed it into a memory. If I drew closer would I be capable of detecting the bad odor which formerly must have existed in all its plentitude and that time, with its terrible footstep which destroys everything, had blurred until it had converted it into an indefinite vapor, an almost anonymous impurity? And if that spot was the result of a vomit, why had he vomited? What spasmodic impulse had caused the materials which were headed for the most absolute and perfect decomposition, to reverse themselves at the point of fulfilling the cycle of our perfect mechanical interior and return to the surface, refusing to cooperate with a system that stands as the one perfect creation of the human body? Why had the food rebelled? Was the mind of man capable of creating something more integral, perfect and synthetic than that which was produced by this long, lank tube, puckered in a multitude of places, in constant movement, and that afterwards expelled the product of its own work to the void? What did the vomit mean? Perhaps it wasn't a rebellion of the food, of the animal maybe, of the pieces of meat that refused to follow the process of absolute decomposition step by step, to which the internal workings of each living being on earth are pledged to subject it. Wasn't excrement and nothing else the authentic creation in our own image and likeness and the true and only product of our genius?

And to think that all that world, all that reality, unique and true, was found in the accumulated filth of that overcoat! I can't say how many hours I spent with my eyes fixed on that one spot over the lapel nor can I remember

60

after so many years the multitude of rich and varied thoughts that occurred in those moments! At the very least I must have passed whole days with my gaze fixed on that undulating, unknown scab. I thought that I could spend a whole lifetime contemplating its uncleanliness and reflecting on it and there was nothing more interesting or significant or sublime or logical on which to pass your time. The other things that men did, all that endless ambitious coming and going, all the search for pleasure (that ended simply in dirty organic secretions of a doubtful odor), all the things that one undertook with measureless enthusiasm, giving their lives at times for them, were pallid replicas of the authentic truth that existed in your own bad odor. Did anything else in the world exist that was capable of producing, reflecting, and transmitting such a plenitude of filth as the human organism? We were the epitome of corruption, the grand product of God himself, and all other intentions were nothing more than the evasion of that cosmic reality. Hygiene, individual and collective, was the most antihuman of creation; and the cities, filthier every day, seemed to anticipate that ultimate state of decomposition against which fruitless efforts are made. The garbage trucks pass and pass again, collecting trash cans of refuse accumulated on the corners, but scarcely twenty-four hours go by than the very same trash cans are already full again of every sort of garbage, as if they never had been emptied. There was always a custodian at work in the streets and in the parks, collecting papers and the leftovers from meals thrown here and there, making the same operation necessary hour after hour, day after day, throughout life, with the same absolute uselessness. Papers and leftovers from meals reappeared instantly as though the city had vomited them—nor did proof of digestion even exist. The subway was always dirty and at times I thought that it was part of an international conspiracy

destined to overthrow (by means of BO) the hygienic pos-
tulates (sound mind in a sound body) of this country. The
huge bridges were always being painted, and one of the
ends that touched the river bank already wore a mantle
of accumulated filth by the time the other end was finished. It was necessary to begin all over again. There were
men who had never done anything else in their lives: to
cap the dirtiness with covers of paint that served no other
purpose than to preserve it, to integrate it with the color,
hide it beneath a surface of temporary luster: the covers
of dust were there: nothing could be done: they formed
the bark of the earth. What wasted expense! What a loss
of time! How beautiful the city would be the day in which
that dried vomit on the overcoat of my friend came back
to life and covered everything in the one sublime reality!
Wouldn't that be, then, the true reign that God has prepared for us?

The world to come was anticipated in the overcoat.
That filth was the powerful magnet that carried me day
after day to the desolate solitude of the park bench; there
I had found company. Needless to say each day the uncleanliness of that overcoat offered me new surprises, as
if the possibilities of decomposition projected toward the
infinite. Human rot was a universe that had the im-
measurable dimensions of space, although it could be enclosed in the magic details of the overcoat. The men of
the park held a fascinating truth, and I had entered its
kingdom.

The spoken word was in no way necessary. The old
man's eyes had great hypnotic power, but there were days
when I hardly looked at him, attracted instead by some
encrustation I had discovered on the overcoat. In any case,
I now found myself submerged in that daily ritual, which
counterbalanced all the emptiness of my life past and present. Would all my future life be absorbed in this way?

Given the direction I was going, I didn't see any other possibility. I didn't want to leave that world and only lamented having to separate myself from it every afternoon for my doubtful encounter with Amanda. I counted the hours that I was separated from the blue overcoat and wished to sleep as soon as possible; sleep shortened the time of my absence. The certainty that the overcoat would be there always, waiting for me, infused my life with a new and unwonted significance.

But the daily separation was a true martyrdom. Generally I lost all sense of time and didn't realize that the afternoon had come to an end and that the return to my apartment cave was inevitable. Worn out from being dragged this way and that by those almost mystical flights, I sometimes lost the notion of myself and was transported by what I would dare to call a nearness to the divine. Maybe I didn't have the right? Perhaps I wasn't learning the lessons of renunciation that had made me reject all human vanities and that caused me to find satisfaction in a crust of old bread? I didn't ask for anything because, although I was not going to be dressed in flowers as the Evangelist proclaimed, but possibly in something else, I knew that God would never abandon me completely since that process that was taking place in me would have to be realized. At all events, how much I hated to separate myself every afternoon from that unique peace that I had found there! The notion of time would shake me suddenly, and I had to make great efforts to get up from the bench. Besides, I felt deeply tired, much more than when I had walked dozens and dozens of blocks during those times (remote for me now) in search of employment. At times, I believe, I had to lean against the walls of houses—so lacking was I in strength. But at the same time I had to pull myself together so that Amanda wouldn't notice that something different was happening to me. She ought not to know because she would be totally incapable of understanding it. How was she going to understand it if she was in a stage of feverish mechanical activity? That microscopic activity was precisely what tired me the most, coming down on me like a tombstone. Even to see her made me more tired and depressed. How distant was Amanda from that world that I—still without freeing myself completely from the remains of vanity in which I had lived—had begun to consider my apostleship.

This devotion made me quickly gain the confidence of the group. At first some looked at me from afar with a certain suspicion, as if I weren't sincere and consequently didn't merit direct, rapid acceptance. I might well be an intruder, someone who infiltrated their sect with unknown motives, a member of some charitable society, a social worker, a religious reformist, a Communist revolutionary, a Protestant minister, even a university student doing an investigation in order to write a doctoral dissertation. Anything was possible. I was in reality much too young (the Benjamin of the group) and my age made me somewhat suspect. I was barely thirty years old and all of them appeared to be past fifty, although I really couldn't say with certainty how old any of them were. Age became so indefinite under the filth that it recalled those women who cover their faces with a thick layer of makeup in their useless passion to conceal their years. Here, without intending it, the opposite effect was gained, and with greater efficacy: that of trying to simulate not a youth they didn't have, but a vague yet legitimate old age. If at that juncture I ran into some "normal" acquaintance, he might possibly have said the years had overtaken me—although naturally he wouldn't have recognized me. There in the park it was known that I wasn't old, but without intending it I merely appeared to be. It was not an affectation on my part. I felt that age in my bones and was glad. Although I lamented that those added years were not authentic, I thought that with daily effort the heavy filth of the centuries would come over me as if I myself were one of those ancient abandoned cathedrals. My entire attitude, all the legitimate intermingling, as I have already indicated, worked to move the most suspicious so that they ceased seeing a stranger in me; I ceased being one thing or the other. In flesh and spirit I became one of them.

They understood that I had another world to which I found myself tied by bonds that were difficult to break. Some of them, perhaps, also had them: wives, children, distant relations. They were obligations acquired in our previous existences when those things appeared essential. There were those, however, who were completely independent, as if they were born out of time, out of space, as if they never had gone further than the park. But they were few. Since the majority had at one time been locked in conditions similar to mine, they waited tranquilly for me to verify that the separation was complete. Besides, they knew from their own experience that the other world would end when its members found it impossible to live with a creature so addicted to his own stench. Was any "normal" being going to be able to approach me if I persisted in that state? The reactions were always the same. The nearest tried reform, but if one offered the proper resistance, they ended by withdrawing, literally covering their noses and fleeing our presence as if we had some Biblical plague. After a certain point it was no longer necessary to make the least effort. Hadn't I noted that in the street no stranger ever came near me to share one of those insipid ideas of "normal" beings with regard to the weather, good or bad? Wasn't it common and usual for the people—in a cafeteria, on the subway, in a waiting room—to separate themselves from "us" as if we were infected, as certainly we were? They were right and that fact was going to segregate us in the most absolute way. But contrary to those who seek integration as a goal, we wanted and preferred to feel ourselves segregated.

When it came to Amanda, I never had to refer to my difficult situation. It was implicit I existed in some such way. Fortunately the increase in production was such that she arrived home later with each passing day, including work every Saturday. Every day she arrived so late at our lodgings that she decided it would be better not to prepare any dinner. I could easily eat something out "there," and she would eat something before coming home. Consequently, when Amanda arrived, I had already dropped into bed and on various occasions pretended to be asleep in order to avoid a conversation that lacked significance. She had developed a habit of febrile and irritating activity which I neither participated in nor witnessed, fortunately, but I could feel it around me even with my eyes closed. What surprised me most was Amanda's attitude with respect to me. I expected some negative reaction regarding the circumstances in which we lived. Especially I feared a reopening of the difficult topic of hygiene since in one sense there existed no possible solution on my part, for I had no intention whatsoever of giving way. But she said nothing. It was as though I were buried in that overcoat which lovingly preserved my uncleanliness, as though the permanence of that bodily corruption was so well tuned that the bad odor that went on accumulating did not reach the surface. Since Amanda hardly saw me in the shadowy apartment (there was not much light, and besides, she avoided turning it on so as not to wake me), she did not have (or did not wish to have) an exact idea of the conditions in which I was living. She finally suggested (and now I thought that she did it in order not to see me) that since the mornings were so cold and since she already knew how to get to the subway, it was definitely unnecessary for me to accompany her. Why was I sacrificing myself in such an unnecessary way? I could sleep in a bit and then go out to look for work (she said in order to say something) later. She behaved as if guided by the most absolute generosity and the greatest disinterest, and this I say in every sense of the word.

She, who had been particularly sensitive to bad odors, appeared not to notice my uncleanliness. That seemed to me inexplicable. Nevertheless, I began to note that when she arrived at the apartment at night, it would be filled with an intense and bothersome odor of the patchouli plant, which came from a cheap perfume that Amanda said they had given her. The perfume was insultingly vulgar, and when it was mixed with my own bad odor it made me nauseous. It appeared to enchant Amanda. Did she use it perhaps to dissociate herself from the olfactory unpleasantness of my presence? Was it that the apartment continued to acquire my odor and she wanted to combat it as though it were a mortal threat? I couldn't say. Besides, Amanda had returned to her time-honored habits of cleanliness. At first she avoided using the bath because it was outside the apartment; she was afraid that someone might assault her in the hall and believed she was going to become ill if she entered that icy bath. But one day she discovered that the shower water was really hot—"enough to pluck chickens"—and decided to try it. Besides, it was Sunday and a friend from the factory had invited her to her house and, later, to the movies. She preferred not to go, especially because I wasn't going, but I considered it a compromise, and perhaps her friend was right when she said Amanda ought to distract herself with something. I, far from raising any objection (because I didn't want to raise any), told her it was a magnificent idea. Then Amanda said that she had to bathe. Without taking off her overcoat (in the hall there was a strong current of air) she went out of the apartment in the direction of the bath. I remained immobile on the bed, expecting the worst. I found myself in a state of panic. It was not, exactly, because of her unexpected outing with an unknown friend. After all, what right had I? Did I have even the remotest to oppose myself to what Amanda might or might not do? I had rights to "nothing." Whatever was Amanda's reality (which was absolutely beyond me), I had no moral authority to intervene in it. Wasn't I happy that her outing allowed me to return to the park precisely on Sunday, the day that no one was expecting me? Wasn't it going to be a motive for general rejoicing? Then, why would I want to question Amanda? But that was not what scared me, rather her sudden return after the bath. I knew that from that moment on any attempt to reach an understanding was going to be impossible and that the opposed directions which the overcoat had delineated—"the overcoats, you mean to say"—would open an irreconcilable gulf between us.

When Amanda returned, a gust of cleanliness swept over the apartment, in spite of the fact that she was wrapped in the overcoat and trembling with cold on account of the chill in the hall, and in the apartment also. It was of such force that for a moment I thought I was strangling. I couldn't breathe. It wasn't the perfume of the soap. It was an allergic reaction to hygiene that caused my asthmatic asphyxia. I went to the window and opened it abruptly, in spite of the cold, and perhaps I was relieved by the eternally worn-out air of the city. Luckily for her, Amanda opened that repugnant vial of perfume with its strong odor of patchouli and the apartment filled with that "fragrance" that was a mask for body odor.

CHAPTER

4

From that moment forth Amanda repeated that troubling Sunday ritual with painful regularity. I suffered it with resignation, covering my head with the overcoat. I had noticed that this operation helped me overcome my allergic reaction and that the progressively bad smell of the overcoat almost completely prevented the intense odor of cleanliness that Amanda exhaled after her bath from passing through the thick weave of the wool. Amanda had once again given way to the most vexing habits of personal hygiene, ignoring the risks of pneumonia or of some disagreeable incident (of a sexual nature) when she came out of the common bath, having seen to it that no particle of dust or dirt remained on her skin. What reason for that useless anxiety over corporal purity? What was she trying to do? What was she trying to preserve? Didn't she realize that in the end she would smell like any other neighbor's daughter? In short, she would have to accept the inevitable. But her cleanliness opposed to my dirtiness continued to create a barrier that would end by separating us completely.

The most surprising aspect of our situation was our paralysis in the face of what was happening. I didn't dare ask Amanda not to bathe. Although it is known that among different animal species the strong odors of the female produce a special excitation in the male, in civilized man it doesn't always work this way and an infinite number of attempts have been made (especially by merchants) to prove the contrary. Animals don't bathe (in the human sense of the word) but maintain their richness of odor (that distinguishes one group from another and avoids confusion), and even man is capable of distinguishing between his personal odor and that of another. But man, carried away by his infinite vanity, bathes, tries to remove from himself the most salient characteristic of his identity. I couldn't share these ideas with Amanda because an ideological abyss separated us. I was sure that she would try to prove the faulty scientific basis of my arguments, bring up such disparate things as birds which bathe in fountains or fish that bathe because they swim in water—the latter being supremely ridiculous. There would be no lack of persons better versed in the sciences who would expound the thesis of the shark, alleging that this ferocious animal (who is certainly no pardoner of lives) spares fish that regularly remove the moss with which the shark is covered. The supposed cleanliness of the cat (which cleans itself with its own saliva) could easily be used as proof, but only by forgetting that saliva is nothing more than another organic secretion (with its odor, certainly) that does nothing more than reaffirm (in its way) the cat's body odor. That would be the same as saying that pigs are clean because they roll in a mudhole—an opinion which could easily be sustained in a contrary sense. None of these ideas passed the borders of my mind. I knew that they ran counter to the concept of civilized hygiene which Amanda had held all her life.

The dispute would have been terrible. If I had told her what I thought (as I actually thought it), that a person who bathes a lot does so because of a tendency to become foul-smelling, she might not have taken the concept as a first premise (Amanda always took things on a personal level), but as a direct allusion. Besides, I had reached such a state that I didn't have strength enough or any wish to change what might possibly be her ideas.

Contrary to what I had anticipated, Amanda no longer gave evidence of disapproval. If I had decided in favor of decomposition, it was not going to be she who stood in my way. She never offered the least reproach regarding the strong odor that issued from my person. Nor did she return to the quasi-humorous nationalistic reference to the piercing odor that had always come from my feet and socks. I, certainly, couldn't tell what she thought about my condition, or if she herself had chosen a different sect, some occult principle within the perfumed confines of her overcoat. Wasn't it logical to think that if I had launched myself toward one world, she had probably chosen another? But a strong barrier of silence separated us. Our most evident counterpoint lay in that dialogue between odors: Amanda responding always with her unalterable bath and with an increasing dose of patchouli that left the apartment impregnated with a kind of sugared pestilence.

Sometimes I was assaulted by the fear of a remote possibility. I sensed Amanda returning from her Sunday ritual and, although I always covered my head, it occurred to me that perhaps she might undress and come to me exhaling perfume through every pore. I saw her inclining toward me, the cleanliness integrated in all the organs of her body, and opening my overcoat wide. But at the same time I told myself that such a fright would never occur. The contact between her pure glossiness and the dirty crust of my body, which continued producing new geological caps day by day, would effect such a repugnance

71

in her that all sexual contact would be impossible. Besides, if I was frightened by such a relationship, wasn't it possible that Amanda lived equally apprehensive of it? In any case, her fear was more logical. Besides my unconventional appearance, wouldn't this mirroring be one of the fundamental reasons why Amanda had distanced herself from me? When she came home late, dead with fatigue, I remember her saying that she'd had a lot of extra work and was in no humor for "anything." Why should I go to the trouble of waiting up for her? No, I need not do it for her sake. It was enough for one of us to sacrifice himself. One day it would be my turn. And she argued strongly in favor of my remaining asleep. Since I had already established the custom of not waking up when she went to work, because "I had never been a friend of the early bird," I realized that frequently whole days passed when we didn't see each other. Perhaps this arrangement calmed her because it made the possibility of a sexual contact remote. I heard her at night walking on tiptoe in order not to wake me (were I awake or asleep) and repeating the same operation in the morning. To the point that since I no longer was looking, I started thinking that it could easily be someone else who entered the apartment, but the strong odor of patchouli argued to the contrary. Nevertheless, wasn't it possible that she spent the nights somewhere else and sent some friend in her place? I told myself no because I had done nothing similar in spite of the fact the opportunity had presented itself. If the apartment was always in a state of semi-darkness and if I practically covered my head with the overcoat, wasn't it possible that someone else could take my place and she not know it? Notwithstanding, I never had done such a thing, which did not mean she wouldn't. Anyway let her do it or not do it, I had to admit I was absolutely ignorant of her world and of the principles which governed it—as she had to be of those that controlled mine. Terrified besides that it might not be her but someone else, I covered my head even more because I was completely certain I didn't want to know it.

Many times nothing like this happened. Amanda was so late that I grew tired of waiting for the sound of the key in the lock and her discreet nocturnal movements. Since with each passing day I ate less well and only enough to keep me on my feet so that I could make it to the park, I lived in a state of perpetual weakness. As soon as I got into bed, that debility became more pronounced and I felt that I went into a kind of faint. My fears regarding Amanda and the desire to evade any contact with her world mixed themselves with my physical condition and the need for my body to recover enough to survive through the following day. For that reason, many times I really did sleep and didn't have to fake it. It was simpler and more convenient. On such occasions (which with each day became more frequent) the estrangement from Amanda grew even greater, more authentic, as if we weren't ourselves, either one of us. All of this implied an absolute acceptance of our circumstances.

Besides the bath, Amanda's outing every Sunday formed part of our accustomed activities. At first she insisted that she would prefer to remain, that if I didn't want her to she was going nowhere, that it was an obligation like any other, that it embarrassed her to say no, that perhaps she needed to distract herself, that it was a psychological expansion, that she had no choice but to accept the invitation, but that if it hurt me she wasn't going. She in reality did not expect any opposition on my part and I, certainly, had no intention of opposing her. Little by little she stopped giving excuses and explanations and her Sunday outing became established like any other of our routine activities, much like her daily work and the extra work that she was always doing, that sham battle where supply never quite kept up with demand. The Sunday outing was not only taking place regularly, but growing longer. The first day she returned early, but little by little like a person feeling out new ground she arrived steadily later, complaining of the enormous distances in the city, the lateness of the trains on Sundays, the insistence of some of her friends that she remain and eat dinner, or whatever other "fantastic" invention. I allowed her to do it, somewhat surprised at the radical change which had come over Amanda—perhaps not realizing that it was no more radical than mine.

Since I seldom looked at her, I didn't know if she had changed physically or in any other outward aspect. I knew that she still used the overcoat and that it fit her equally badly, but that she took special care of it, so much so that it almost seemed an intentional effort on her part to distance herself from me. I think she had acquired some new clothes, but since I continued with the ones I'd brought and always had them on, never changing, I had no reason to open the closet door, where possibly she kept her new garments—if she really had any. I felt very little curiosity to verify these things. It seemed to me she had changed her hairdo, although she still wore that same black thing on her head—or something very similar. Which is to say, outwardly, as seen from the corner of my eye, she didn't appear to have changed much although I imagined that "inwardly" (I mean, inside the overcoat) fundamental changes had taken place. Her aseptic body "lived" abundantly under that uninviting exterior. A distant anxiety that she existed further from me would come and attack me at times, but I scared it away as if it were part of a weakness in my former life which I had to eradicate in favor of a more authentic existence. In spite of that outward appearance that I supposed was little altered, and

74

notwithstanding the fact I scarcely looked at her, there shone through (perhaps because of that uncharacteristic taste for cheap perfume) a vulgarity that was, I would say, quite foreign to her, but now was firmly rooted. Perhaps she was the victim of some contagious disease that she couldn't escape? Was it the gulf of her "sickness" that separated her from "mine"?

At bottom I didn't want to know anything. What I wanted to do was to fulfill my destiny completely, and the most authentic thing in my life was my daily immersion in the park. Every morning I marched toward it with a sense that I was performing a religious act. There the other overcoat awaited me and the long conversations took place. I call my long monologues conversations, although they took place with one or another spot of grease on his overcoat, that and the exchange of enigmatic glances that went from the depths of my eyes to the depths of his. And the sad thing was that I could discover nothing (no reply) in them. I believe we never said anything, one to the other, and our "chats" were always occasions for silence.

Although we did not speak and although in reality an atmosphere of withdrawal commonly reigned in the park, there were moments of abrupt and inexplicable animation. Some of those who gathered there were really consummate talkers and they spent the day musing over something, generally to themselves. It was like a distant prayer, subliminal, in which words could not be understood but had the constancy of a lament. At times everyone seemed to be listening, creating a silence even more marked save in those who appeared to be directing the prayer. But the most authentic talkers (in the usual sense of the word) were those that always came with some of the latest news, toward which they would take various attitudes. These were the spokesmen of reality and those who maintained a more direct contact with public life. The only trouble was that such contact was at bottom in conflict with our existence since it admitted the world toward which they made reference.

It's necessary to clarify all this. For example, from time to time there would appear without previous notice one of those "spokesmen of reality" with news that he classified as "up-to-the-minute." The "up-to-the-minute news" was awaited by some with the greatest anguish. Others assumed an attitude of scorn, as if they knew it all already and felt the most profound disdain for those revolutionaries and hotheads. Without doubt they had still not reached a state of putrefied "grace." The majority, those who had a greater maturity and had experienced more years in accumulating that gratuitous disintegration (the patriarchs of solitude), adopted an attitude of indifference that was frequently accompanied by a certain condescension for those who still felt the painful lashes of chaos. This "up-to-the-minute news" was anything whatever, except the latest news it pretended to be. These activist misfits, possibly former men of action who tried uselessly to adjust themselves to the credo of the park, to its daily corruption, found themselves assaulted without warning by remote explosions of what they once had been. It was if a recurrent trauma took place on passing from attacks of action to retreats into paralysis. When those who passed lives of slow but certain putrefaction looked backwards in time, they were shaken by tremors that caused them to seek escape valves. This condition created moments of crisis in the park, as if a gust of reality had suddenly jolted them.

The jolting was false, nevertheless. An old man who had lost an arm in the war claimed that the Japanese would never dare to start a world war. The war that ended in Hiroshima, with the explosion of the atomic bomb, didn't follow the proper chronology; for many the attack on Pearl Harbor took place years after the atomic explosion over Hiroshima. They had come to the conclusion that the atomic bomb which exploded over Hiroshima would have precluded an attack on Pearl Harbor; or, the reverse, that the Japanese would attack the naval base because of the bombing of Hiroshima. Some who had seen hair-raising action said that they would refuse to be recruited into a war in which they had already participated. There was no lack of tricksters; since the deeds were already accomplished fact, they could appear prophetic simply by pretending ignorance and finding someone foolish enough to deny their position. It was like anticipating the birth of Christ and the advent of Christianity (facts known to everyone) after their actual occurrence, but pretending to have foreseen these events. There were times in which, day after day, someone evoked a certain period that he wanted to relive. The hardships of the economic depression of the thirties became immediate reality and the problems of scarcity and unemployment were discussed, measures adopted, and solutions sought, all of which had long been accomplished fact. Other times it was a fear of the "Chicago gangsters," and the individual lived in a state of constant alarm, expecting gunfire at any moment. A high point was reached when they spoke of laws related to the prohibition of alcoholic beverages. The dry law signaled the end of the world. The drunks broke their silence and began to shout that the evil-smelling gin was life itself and that they would prefer death before having it yanked from their hands. The desperation gave way to chaos. The war returned, and while some cried that they wouldn't go (and showed some mutilated limb that "now" was not there because that was just the place they lost it) and wouldn't send their sons to certain death (sons they never had or that they had "already" lost in the war), others asked for machine guns and grenades in order to go out and kill Germans and Japanese. A climate of violence took over the park: some were made desperate by the crisis of the depression, others by deaths on the fields of battle. Some were violent in their opposition to the government, others defended it with their fists. Then the sanest, those who always maintained calm or showed indifference, those who had withdrawn deep into their own eye sockets (the patriarchs of solitude) intervened, trying to calm in some way the desperate and the possessed. Generally the dates didn't make much difference, and the fact that a war was over was no guarantee they were not going to die in it. Those of Jewish blood were sure that Hitler would win the war and that they would be placed in concentration camps and would end their days in the gas chamber. It was difficult to convince them that Hitler was dead. They were sure he was still alive, and I came to think they might be right.

Anything whatever might give rise to one of these episodes that poisoned our tranquility. Someone stumbled on some old newspaper in his digs, some headline of twenty, thirty, forty years earlier. He gave it new life, transporting it in time, which once again became the present. Those who lived more in the present dug among the tin cans in the trash and found news of the previous week, of the month just past, and turned it into an "up-to-the-minute" occurrence. Chronological order was not respected: Hitler comitted suicide before coming to power. The peace treaty was signed before war was declared. Any chance event could break the equilibrium.

They expected the worst (when already it had been years since the worst had happened) and they expounded all sorts of theories about coming events. They took sides, engaging in violent discussions. Some talked of events that never would take place, imaginary battles, upsets, nonexistent victories. They insulted each other, made peace, came to blows: all without order or mutual understanding. The wars lasted a couple of days until someone, luckily, found some old magazine where a peace had been signed.

This "illness of being alive" was one of the saddest characteristics of the group. It meant, simply, that in spite of our deep faith in dissolution, we might "backslide" at any moment. The "illness of being alive" was the only sickness that really existed, the maddening confirmation that we were here. At such times I seemed to find traces of sorrow in their eyes. Their eyes hesitated in the depths of their night, sparkling uncertainly as if they were red-hot coals. What a painful experience it was to listen to that grotesque chorus of voices clamoring for me to participate. They were a reflection of myself. Their eyes went deeper yet and I thought they would disappear entirely, as if the riddle had been brutally attacked by a detective's arrogant objectivity. But neither he nor I showed the least sign of commotion. We remained motionless (more motionless than ever) as if we feared that the "illness of being alive" was a contagious disease capable of attacking us treacherously. I was afraid. And I imagined then the antiseptic nudity of Amanda. I wanted them to all grow quiet at once and to restore the peace of that sanctuary. Why weren't measures taken to avoid the disruption of order? Wasn't observing our putrefaction the one authentic mission here on earth? I, I believe, questioned them with my eyes and was filled with infinite pity, for it was impossible to deny those sick creatures the ultimate consolation of the faith. They were pitiful dropouts and some were condemned to the hell of never being able to rise above it. It was the fire of life that would not let them rot and that rebelled against the imminent corruption of the flesh. The "illness of being alive" moved through the group for a while, but as if it carried within itself the seeds of its own natural pathology it ended in a heavy fatigue, in a profound disappointment. Those who had excited themselves the most seemed to collapse heavily at the end, overthrown by the absurdity of a life that couldn't be, that was a pathological expression of the flesh. The calmest triumphed, those who contemplated their residue and the accumulation of residue upon residue.

These discussions contained besides, a fascinating paradox within their absurd chronology. The violence they awoke and the events they forecast contrasted with the final results. It was as if we saw the events again by hindsight and realized the smallness of our emotions and the uselessness of our agitation. An article in the press that seemed to anticipate the end of the world and that produced intense alarm in us (such as was re-experienced in the park) ended simply in nothing. In the altered chronological order there was an ultimate truth: peace was signed before war was declared. Although historically it was not the same that Pearl Harbor began a war instead of ending it, in the last analysis it was the same. That convinced me that the only possible reality was my own. The other was, actually, part of the "illness of being alive."

How had I escaped this disease? I feared it, feared the contagion, feared that it might overtake me soon. I watched those eyes in the depths of their universe as if asking them if it was written that I should escape the disease or if something very different had been spoken there (in that universe). But I found no reply, only the riddle itself. The eyes showed astonishment, however, at my state of faith. In a short time I had achieved what had taken others years to acquire. My immersion in the overcoat had been absolute, my devotion to the corruption of the flesh a commitment without strings, my search in the scab of the overcoat a mystical ascension. But I must not let myself be carried away by the vanity of the elected. Might it not be precisely because of that unmerited completeness that I could be punished, fall unexpectedly into sin and lose the possibility of reaching the abundance of the Kingdom and the ultimate results of grace?

I had to reaffirm myself. If we are secretions of the flesh, I ought, then, to reaffirm myself in the products of my own body. I allowed my urine to dampen my thighs and my legs. It moistened my skin and my clothing, went through my pants and left its chemical track on the overcoat. I promised myself the sacrifice of always making water in my pants.

The manifestations of the "illness of being alive" left a heavy mark on our environment. We felt we had been crushed, although individually we might not have experienced it. The stillness gathered little by little after those moments. We were even more silent, remaining motionless before the emptiness. We looked at each other quietly and let time pass over us. We contemplated our overcoats. The spots formed scaly arabesques that irritated the fingertips. With closed eyes we toured the arid surfaces of the wool. A blindman could also follow the corrugations of those surfaces as if they were maps in relief. The filth wasn't even and each instant we felt the fluctuations of history. We hardly moved our fingers, as if wishing to prolong that moment for eternity. As we pressed, we discovered new mysteries of loathsomeness and were transported. Thus, very slowly, sight, touch and smell reported the panorama of our organic decomposition. Because smell also tried to capture, in addition to the eyes and the fingers, the nuances of those spots that carried olfactory signatures. We specialized, trying to collect the olfactory chiaroscuro of rot, the infinite frontiers of one odor with another, the distinctive characteristics of each stench.

Every afternoon when I separated myself from my world and neared the apartment that I shared (?) with Amanda, I asked myself how long this nonexistent relationship would last. I promised myself to end it that very night, but as always I covered my head with the overcoat and barely heard Amanda's discreet footsteps that avoided all noise, and I never said anything. I thought that Amanda posed a latent danger and at any moment might evoke an evil memory. More than her body, it was the persistence of her love that worried me. Once I had said to her: "love lives beyond lies and false scruples." There was always the risk that that love might impose itself like an "illness of being alive," capable of short-circuiting the new order to which my existence was dedicated.

Every afternoon when I returned from the park I had to pass by "The Great Department Stores." I looked at the huge illuminated showcases that exhibited manikins in the latest styles—not because I felt the least attraction toward them, but because I preferred to conduct what I called "exercises of indifference." I told myself that I ought to look at them and that the reaffirmation of my person would take the form of an inner rejection—I would be fooling myself if I tried to evade such circumstances. My glance passed over them, perceiving only spots of color, an abstraction that for me had not the least significance. Consequently I was able to conquer with relative ease a certain suspicion I had of "The Great Department Stores."

One day, on allowing my gaze to run over one of those window displays, I was struck by an irregular abstraction formed by the letters on a typewriter keyboard—qwertyuiopasdfghjklñzxcvbnm. I looked fixedly at that disorder as if to discover some underlying reason—qwertyuiopasdfghjklñzxcvbnm. What could be the meaning of that absurd arrangement that corresponded to no phonetic order and related to no idea? I contemplated it in its emptiness—qwertyuiopasdfghjklñzxcvbnm—noticing how the whiteness of the letters was outlined by the blackness of the keys. The word touched me with its musical significance, for it produced a kind of "sorrow of life." I wanted to evade it, but my eyes remained fixed on that evocation—qwertyuiopasdfghjklñzxcvbnm—that attacked me suddenly, not very intensely, but enough to upset me. How was it possible that an abstraction could touch me in this way? I told myself it made no sense, but while I looked at it—qwertyuiopasdfghjklñzxcvbnm—I felt it boring into my consciousness and wanted to forget everything else. Perhaps one could create a melody if he disposed adequately of that disarranged alphabet? I looked at the letters in reverse and they jostled me again: mnbvcxzñlkjhgfdsapoiuytrewq. It was a wound because undoubtedly those letters were trying to communicate something, begging a musical order even though it might turn out discordant. I looked at them fixedly but with the clear inner notion that I didn't want to hear them, that although they clamored from their keyboard for the company of my fingers I was closed to their voices, which wouldn't be much more than a senseless and rhythmic tock-tock, the hollow tum-tum of a drum that says nothing.

This encounter in "The Great Department Stores" increased my confidence in myself since I believed it increased my control over forgetfulness. Sometimes I stopped to look in one of those large mirrors, and each day I recognized myself less. The "deconstruction" of my being was the greatest of all my creations and there couldn't be another which would better it. I didn't see myself, rather the process of a putrefaction to which I contributed day after day. My somber emaciated face gave evidence of a permanent five o'clock shadow that was nothing more than my usual bad shave. I always did it with an old, slightly rusty knife that lent a happy consistency to my ineptness. My sunken eyes revolved in the depths of their sockets and my face returned the loathsome smile of my own riddle. The overcoat shone in its filth under the lights of "The Great Department Stores." I remained contemplating it for some time, discovering new spots, recalling its putrefaction. Each day the spoilage increased and the speed with which it happened was surprising. Who would guess, seeing me covered with that thick pestilential crust, that I'd only worn it a few months in my priestly calling? It was clear that my situation was unique and that in the park they had immediately recognized qualities of the elect in me. Elected of the carrion, my dedication was making quick and far-reaching inroads into my being, advancing me step by step toward annihilation. How was it that those passers-by, so greedy in the collection of minutiae, didn't stop to contemplate me (and to contemplate the overcoat) as the most authentic and supreme of the manikins? They didn't do it possibly because I made them remember themselves—I was the authentic lament of their own keyboard and they preferred not to listen to it.

But one day, before that same mirror which gave back my reflection, there occurred a frighteningly unpleasant incident that caused me to withdraw from the image I observed there. It was like those superimposed images we see in the movies where one becomes mixed with another. Just when I was most concentrated in my devotional contemplation, the mirror gave back another reflection which I was not prepared for. Next to the overcoat (almost on top of it) was reflected a manikin in a wedding gown. It was a re-creation of the nuptial moment "by overcoat," and I turned my head violently in order not to see it. I saw, nevertheless, the bridal dress which the manikin exhibited in the window, in all its lacy fullness. Amanda herself reappeared. But more than Amanda was the gown (that gown which had been left behind) which for a moment (only for a moment) awoke emotions which I considered dead. With my hand I warded off that sentimental allegory, as you would a fly, and I managed to resist making such an equivalence. I mustn't let myself be carried away by a nonexistent wedding dress, I thought. To cap it all, while I was looking at the wedding gown which had remained behind, another overcoat superimposed itself heavily, wrapping it in a heat that was alien to Amanda and which did not fit the white purity of the gown. It was an immense rabbit-skin coat (I believed) that was made up of thick pieces of pelt in vertical strips. The vast multiplication of brown rabbits reached downward, hiding the figure of the woman who was reflected for a moment in the glass of the showcase. The skins reached almost to her ankles and some black boots which served as feet for the strange animal. Its head was covered by a black rag, and since nothing "human" was visible I can only say that I "supposed" it belonged to the female sex. Through an association of ideas I can't explain, perhaps because of the way it walked or from that black thing it wore on its head, or for having been reflected momentarily on the glass that let me see, further off, the wedding dress which had remained behind, I related Amanda to those disembodied images. True recognition was impossible because the woman (I believed it was) had her back to me and was going away, besides which I could find nothing "personal" about her. It was absurd for me to relate her to Amanda since Amanda still used (I believed) that deformed black overcoat which once had been the companion of mine. But I realized I couldn't be sure of any such thing since I hadn't seen Amanda since time immemorial for reasons already explained, namely the covering of my head with the overcoat from before she arrived at the apartment until after she left. Consequently Amanda could easily have acquired a new overcoat which might well consist of multiple rabbit skins. The idea seemed absurd to me, and if I hadn't been so tired perhaps I would have followed those hurried steps—she moved as if wishing to reach some destination soon. Besides, I didn't want to let myself be carried away by an excitement which should simply be ignored. Also, the woman was accompanied. The gloved hand of a man supported her arm, imprisoning those unhappy animals. He was a strong man and tall, with wide shoulders, who wore a short black leather jacket. He had no hat and I believed I could distinguish from afar the lustrous white hair of someone a bit libidinous and repulsive to me, "naturally."

I don't know how much time passed. During that interval I had seen a succession of images that moved me, as if I never would be free of that "illness of being alive." But my mission was to leave it all behind, and whether Amanda was this or that to me it ought not to matter. The newest possibility was even more dangerous than the momentary recollection of the wedding dress she had left behind. I was doing too well to let myself be carried away by jealousy. I turned toward the bridal gown and looked at it head-on, focusing on the transparent lace. The showcase window protected it from dust and I felt a cloying sweetness in my mouth. I could take it or leave it because all it caused me was a nausea that wrenched my stomach, and without much effort I produced an unpleasant belch.

I ought to say that I considered the battle against sexuality as won. From the moment that Amanda had turned into an overcoat with some legs that might well be of wood and lost herself in the bowels of the subway, the disappearance of her body favored the annihilation of sex. I can't deny that the "existence" of Amanda's body in the apartment was a latent danger that could trigger a negative reaction at any moment. Instinct is a painful sign of life that carries odious consequences. Nevertheless, in the long run the terrifying experience in the urinal contributed very favorably to my purposes, especially since the terror was so great that I decided not to confront it. From that moment on, my hand avoided all contact with that part of my body, and the decision to let those chemical substances I produced accumulate on me contributed greatly to that sense of emasculation. The contrast with Amanda's neatness increased my security (and possibly hers), since a sexual relationship between beings so different was like sexual relations between animals of different species. Besides that atrophied eroticism, the cheap perfume which seemed to have seduced Amanda (a trait which to me was inexplicable) produced in me an olfactory rejection bordering on nausea. It was impossible to cross the barrier of that perfume and arrive at the odor of her body, an intimate secretion that very well might have been dangerous. But I didn't remember it (nor did I wish to), confronted as I was by the tranquilizing opposition of patchouli. Amanda's body seemed covered with that perfume as though it were part of her skin. I personally succeeded in ridding certain parts of my body of all erotic significance. It occurred to me that this was what all "authentic" priests should do and I thought, after all, it's only a urinary tract. In this way my brain discarded all conscious sexuality. By will power I succeeded in eliminating the instinct of that state of consciousness (if I don't contradict myself), but from time to time I saw myself regressing toward the eroticism of adolescence and felt myself dampened by wet dreams. This mortified me, although the idea that another secretion was uniting with the other creations of my body helped compensate for that feeling of "life" which tried to gain ground through the avenue of my subconscious.

As the reader will have guessed, I decided against any fixed course of action, including that moment when I could have used the rabbit-skin overcoat as the logical basis for a rupture which surely Amanda would have welcomed. Nor did I even dare to confirm the truth about said overcoat.

When I arrived at the apartment, Amanda had still not returned, a thing that I feared, for if Amanda was the woman in the rabbit-skin coat there would have been time for her to reach our room. At all events, she might easily have gone somewhere else, "naturally." Since the last thing I wanted was a scene marked by jealousy, which seemed to me like the most miserable of all the "illnesses of being alive," I decided to go to bed and cover my head with the overcoat, "naturally." I heard the steps of "that woman" in the hall, the sound of the key as it was placed in the lock, the squeak of the door as it opened. Terrified, like a small boy imprisoned by a frightening and fearful darkness, I stuck my head in the pillow so as to see nothing, and in the midst of that infinite terror I went to sleep.

On the morning of the following day there occurred an unexpected incident (of a character anything but fantastic) on which I had in no way counted. During the night a heavy snowfall had taken place and the city appeared completely covered by an immense mantle of snow. When I opened my eyes Amanda—"that woman"—had already gone and the apartment was in complete darkness. I had tilted my head slightly, but I still didn't get up because I wanted to be completely sure the apartment was vacant. It was hard for me to move, for I was accustomed to sleeping in a state of utmost rigidity. This rigidity began by being artificial (so that Amanda would believe I was sleeping when I really wasn't) but was now fairly natural, to the extent that each night I slept with the most total immobility, as if my presence would pass unnoticed even by myself. On getting up, my movements were sluggish and my joints creaked as if they belonged to an arthritic. It was clear I was sinking into immobility, for except for the short distance from my room to the park I got no other exercise. While lying in the room and sitting in the park, my movements were minimal. In any case, this is secondary in comparison to the events which I now had to confront. Certain of Amanda's absence, I got up and went to the window. An intense light made me close my eyes. I opened them with a certain foreboding and contemplated the thick mantle of snow on the rooftops. Everything seemed wrapped by a blinding and insupportable whiteness that hurt my eyes just to look at it. The blue heavens glittered without a single cloud to interrupt their "perfect" coloration. Although I couldn't see the sun from the window, its brilliance was visible everywhere. But the cold was intense. Fortunately the chimneys of the city were all working well and the gray smoke seemed to anticipate the dark particles that, little by little, ceaselessly, would interrupt that "perfect" whiteness. I longed for shadows. I looked for my dark glasses and luckily they cast a gray tint over the white and the blue, making them more tolerable. It was as if the crystal of my lenses covered everything with a mantle of dust that was in my eyes. In the same way that the odor of Amanda's clean body produced a shortness of breath that almost choked me, the white brilliance of things or the consciousness of their clarity blinded me.

Immediately I realized a terrible fact that was for me, in these moments, like the end of the world. The park benches would also be covered with snow and surely it would be impossible to sit on them to converse, as was our custom. I call conversing my monologues in front of the overcoat and the intersection of enigmatic glances holding an infinite number of questions that embrace an infinite number of possibilities. I put on some old boots that Amanda's companions at work had given her, thinking perhaps they would work for me. Although they were large for me and only helped to increase my grotesque appearance, I used them—perhaps precisely for that reason, although it is equally certain I had nothing else to wear. Then I left the apartment in a state of uncertainty and desperation, as if the future of my life might be at stake in these moments. It turned out that it was, although I would only learn that much later. Unfortunately there was no way of hurrying. To my chronic fatigue and the stiffness of my movements (especially during the morning) was added the climatological reality of the city. In some places the snow came to my knees and in others the cement of the sidewalk or the asphalt had a covering of ice which made it almost impossible to walk without falling. Actually, I fell two times. In the cross streets the traffic was practically paralyzed and the automobiles were all covered with snow. Those that moved at all came slowly like apparitions. The avenues that ran from north to south and were the vital arteries of the city had been partially cleared. Here the traffic was more intense, and the snow began to mix itself with the dirt characteristic of the area, forming a species of gray slush that was more real than that dissonant whiteness in a world of perennially dirty rooftops.

When I arrived at the corner from which I could spot the park, I registered its frightening desolation. It was as though the park had disappeared. Everything was covered with snow and I could hardly pick out the silhouettes of the benches. Only the bare black branches of the trees gave evidence of what had been. Not even human footprints broke the curved perfection of the snow. It was as though no one had ever been there. All would have been bearable if I had spotted at least an overcoat. But there was absolutely nobody there. What was going to become of me? Where could I turn? Would I have the courage to go back on the trail of a job that didn't exist and that they never would offer me? Was I always going to be abandoned? I was falling again into a vacuum. I understood that my life had been filled with significance and that suddenly that significance had left me. I didn't know what to do. My entire organism rebelled against a possibility that I wouldn't accept. It seemed that I was in the midst of a polar or Siberian country sunk in snow, buried in it, alone. I ceased looking at the buildings (still gray) in the background and saw only that white brilliance of the snow. I walked a short distance and arrived at one of the corners of the park. Rigid, I was the replica of those men of the past who have been changed into statues. But I was not budging from here. I preferred turning into a block of ice to recognizing the absence of the others. I was ready for the most complete annihilation and was not going to retreat. I couldn't go back to Amanda. She "already was a thing of the past." The layers of my corruption had been forming on the overcoat I wore, my only possible creation; and I was not about to compromise or deny my one emblem of success. I thought for the briefest moment about the other *I* that had aspired to things, including creating them in a burst of fantasy. There was nothing save our own decomposition. And that disintegration which had found company in disintegration; no, I was not going to retreat just because the weather had taken a turn for the worse. I was rotting and I loved my putrefaction above all things, and there was even a religion of decomposition in which I was not alone. I believed in the Almighty Decomposition. And if the reign of heaven existed, the only possible reign was that of decomposition. This was the religion that Amanda did not share with me, devoted to daily hygiene (which was her rite), her thermos (that was her chalice) and her cheap perfume (which was her blood). These were the touchstones of her earthly existence. But not mine. I advanced toward the park where there wasn't a single overcoat. I entered it as one enters a desert or a tundra, great words that I only knew in the desolation of my chest. Everything was snow. The snow there was more frighteningly white, as if it radiated a light that blinded me beyond my glasses. How cruel nature could be! Everything could be wrecked by a stupid fickle gesture, as if a badly brought-up child, frivolous and haughty, decides on destruction because he has nothing else to do. The same force that had sent that snow could have sent an earthquake or a volcanic eruption, drawing flames from the center of the earth and throwing forth the ferocious decomposition that gave it pleasure. It vomited over us the leftovers of its digestion and left them on its skin to form the geological crusts. Between those crusts we were the parasites, the lice and the fleas of its ultimate crop. We covered the earth like desperate wingless bugs that vainly tried to penetrate a mantle with the solidity of the ages. And the earth, with that wisdom we lacked, wasn't even bothered by our efforts. We were voracious pubic lice that destroyed one another, grew stale and sickly in our round, built the layers of that monster and were tormented in the body of a God that had no desire to intervene save to bury us in the middle of one of His spasms. How loathsome was that nature which could mash us with a backhand slap and when it had the courtesy not to do so moved us in such a way as to give it thanks! But if the easiest thing was destruction, I would not be the one to oppose its work which, after all, would be far more accomplished than the deeds of the wingless insects. And the others? What had become of them? Had they disappeared, swallowed by that snow? Perhaps they were here, buried beneath that mantle? Wasn't it possible that nature had taken them by surprise and had covered them with that white sudarium that sounded so poetic and was so much ours? I ran through the park and launched myself toward the part where I thought lay the bench on which we had so often sat in our overcoats. I saw those eyes in the depths of their sockets covered by a mantle of transparent snow, but hard as diamonds. I was sure they were hidden there somewhere, staring up from a bench or from the cement itself. There had been a frosty massacre that had spilled blood which was congealed in great red splotches. I wanted to escape, but the snow wouldn't let me, and I fell again and again. At times the snow almost covered me, my body extended horizontally on top of it. I was like a man walking through a polar landscape where there is no beginning or end, point of departure or goal. So white was everything. I had lost the notion of the city, almost the notion of the park, and only the vague sense of a black tree trunk entered my brain as a possible reference point in the white. But I felt that my skull itself had congealed, that it was a block with cerebral convolutions incapable of thought. Consequently I had lost the power to move toward heat; rather the influence of frost in my head carried me toward cold. It was as if my skull, because of the weight of ice, bore me down. It was at this point that those indecipherable letters returned like an alphabet of ice: qwertyuiopasdfghjklñzxcvbnm. They meant something, but they were also frozen and could represent nothing more than their own chilliness. They were congealed into a Mona Lisa riddle. I saw them—qwertyuiopasdfghjklñzxcvbnm— and if I had been able to move I would have touched them, but I had the feeling it would be useless because they would break at the least touch. The search for them began

93

once again in my head, and I finally fell on the point that I arbitrarily decided was the target. I began to scratch in the snow without knowing if I was looking for a grave or digging my own. The letters meanwhile broke in my own frozen skull, producing the sound of fine and fragile crystal that shatters into a thousand unimportant pieces. They fled toward outer space, sparkling in the distance like an unreachable world, broken and disintegrated. They distanced themselves one from the other, separated by thousands of years and rejecting all possibility of meaningful reunion. My hands that might have touched them once and given them definite content, now opened graves in the snow. Sunk in their midst, I saw long grave-like trenches full of the unburied corpses of a great war. It was the large common grave of those who had no other, of those who are machine-gunned in the trenches, of those who are shot against thick walls; letters that were never going to reunite to form a single word, not even . . . "n . . . o . . . n . . . e . . ." These thoughts came and went in frozen blocks, exact quadrangles like the cubes of ice we throw in a glass. They went, they melted, and nevertheless they froze again in space in order to come back at me as if they were returning phantasms. A white lace drew near within the ice, but as it did so across a thousand light years it acquired the yellowness of time, arriving as frozen dust ready to disintegrate at any moment. My mind couldn't think in a cold which made reasoning impossible. The realization, nevertheless, that they had been victims of an avalanche and were there below that white massacre, came and went rhythmically. I was sure that they were there, lamenting that only I had been abandoned, scratching not to dig them out of their graves, but to allow myself to die with them. There would lie the cadaver in the overcoat with that vomit which spelled the eternity of man and was a microscopic expression of the eternity of God.

And that vomit was mine because it was I myself. If the destruction had been consummated, let it be consummated in me; and I sought it while my hands congealed to the point that they were taking on a painful rigidity. This rigidity was a little different from my daily experience on the bed. That was (I believed even in the middle of sleep) a conscious rigidity, a voluntary act, a painful contraction that altered the muscles and even the bones, but this now had nothing to do with my will, but was imposed from without. Rather than contraction there was possession, and even a kind of relaxation that turned rigid again, not from contracting but owing to the freezing of my tissues. It was like an invasion before which one could do nothing because one was completely disarmed. My body horizontal in the snow, almost buried by it, I lay at full length while my hands made a pretense of digging in the ice. The cold was so intense that I felt myself being turned into a solid block. My overcoat had completely lost the transitory function for which it had been created, and I felt myself frozen inside of it as if my coffin were a great block of ice that made movement impossible. I was dead, but I could smell that climax of ultimate fetidness as if my entire being had been externalized in universal corruption. But little by little that fetidity was being lost, according to the degree that freezing took over. While I moved toward congelation I thought that perhaps that cold wasn't destruction, but conservation. The tips of my fingers stopped moving. They were also buried next to me in great blocks of ice under the snow. Our decomposed organisms and our overcoats in the process of decomposition would be preserved in an eternity of frost. On the day of judgment our corruption would come forth from its frozen state like a Frankenstein monster revived, and we would inherit the only kingdom possible to putrefaction, the burial of our resurrected rot. I prayed as I went. It was a mechanical prayer of frozen phrases that shattered in the air . . . I believe in decomposition/ Almighty God . . . work thy/ decomposition and thy/ decomposition be done . . . De/ composition are you/ and unto decompo/ sition you will return . . . Only the decompos/ ed will enter into the kingdom of de/ composition . . . I believe in the de/ composition of the/ body . . . the decom/ position . . . everlasting . . . De . . . com . . . po . . . si . . . tion . . . re . . . sur . . . rect . . . ed . . . the . . . words . . . con . . . geal . . . ed . . . in . . . the . . . de . . . comp . . . po . . . si . . . tion . . . and . . . mov . . . ed . . . slow . . . ly . . . like . . . phan . . . tasms . . . a . . . d . . . i . . . s . . . t . . . i . . n . . c . . t . . i . . m . . . a . . . g . . . e . . . o . . . f . . . a . . . n . . . o . . . v . . . e . . . r . . . c . . . o . . . a . . . t . . . a . . . p . . . p . . . e . . . a . . . r . . . e . . . d . . . w . . . i . . . t . . . h . . . i . . . n . . . a . . . f . . . r . . . o . . . z . . . e . . . n . . . b . . . l . . . o . . . c . . . k . . . q . . . w . . . e . . . r . . . t . . . y . . . u . . . i . . . o . . . p . . . a . . . s . . . d . . . f . . . g . . . h . . . j . . . k . . . l . . . ñ . . . z . . . x . . . c . . . v . . . b . . . n . . . m . . . ???????????????????

CHAPTER
5

My eyes were closed, but I was perfectly aware that I had come back to reality. I couldn't say where, however. Nor could I say what I had been doing before entering that void from which I seemed to be returning. It wasn't that I had lost my memory, it was that my memory had still not come out of that congealed state to permit a harmonious reorganization of thought. The bad odors hovered near me with their accustomed familiarity, and I felt I was wrapped as if by old friends you encounter in the regions of smell. This consciousness of odor made me realize I had taken the first steps toward unthawing. My thoughts (I felt it) tried to form themselves little by little like parts of an icy picture puzzle that is found in outer space. I realized that I still had eyes, but I couldn't open them, first of all because I had the feeling I couldn't see. In the second place I knew perfectly well that if I opened my eyes they were going to break, and I saw them divided under my eyelids in a hundred crystalized particles that still preserved their original form, but would come apart at the least movement. I saw them so clearly within my blindness: the eye was a square that I contemplated through a microscope, or it was as if I saw it through that perfect circular focus of an occulist's lens. I knew, besides, that the globe of the eye was completely frozen and that therefore the ducts serving the retina couldn't function. The retina had suffered a contraction because of the cold, and it was going to be necessary to repair it with a little silicone. The closed eyelids weighed heavily with the terrible frigidity of a marble tombstone covering a grave, but the consciousness that they were protecting destructible flesh, fragile laminates of ice, also argued in favor of leaving them closed. In any case, within that frigidity and blindness there was an indefinite sensation of heat in this place I found myself, that was primarily olfactory. I was sure the warmth proceeded directly from the existence of materials in decomposition. There was a cold current of air I couldn't recognize, carrying distant intimations that frightened me: the odor of cheap perfume . . . bath soap . . . simple cleanliness. It aroused the feeling, I suppose, of an unexpected pneumonia. But the throb of the heat, which was like a fever, but wasn't, calmed me, although my stiffness was such that if there existed some uneasiness it was remote and subconscious, since my nerves could hardly function. What I'm telling can't be taken as exact testimony without referring to the transformation on which it is based, since it's impossible for me to say what it is to be frozen when I felt nothing. In any case, I believe that decomposition began again in the respiratory tract because of an inflow of oxygen. It was evidently the worn-out air that gave me the life I believed was lost. I smelled of death and the only contact I could establish lay in the remembered odor of some rotting animal that I had smelled once, possibly in open country. In this way I had a familiarity with the odor, that in spite of its being foreign was now part of my being. But the curious part of all this was that the odor was not part of my death, but of my life. I felt a kind of progression as it increased that recalled times at home (as a boy) when some savory dish excited my appetite. It was obvious that the odor whetted an appetite in me: an appetite for my own putrefying flesh (that was a kind of self-cannibalism), the appetite to live. This made me think I wasn't dead, that the process had reversed. I clearly detected the thawing of the *BO*, which was essential to the recovery of life and that gave me a feeling of warmth that increased little by little. Instinctively I was recognizing the odors and separating them as one separates (on painting them on a piece of paper) the colors of the rainbow. The prism of decomposition returned me to life. In this way I realized that I had sweated copiously. How was it that I could have done such a thing, given the low temperature to which I had been subjected? The consciousness of sweat didn't come to me (yet) as a tactile phenomenon, but as a vague olfactory sensation. This change also gave me confidence. Over the stink of death (of a rotten, unburied animal) was imposed the vital fetidness of a functioning organism. Because sweat is the characteristic pestilence of the man of action, the athlete, and I had it in every pore of my body. This odor was growing stronger little by little, dominant, as though I were an immense armpit. But at the same time I did not exclude other secretions that surged here and there, remote at times, until they reached the first level of consciousness, receding at times, rhythmically, as if part of a symphonic counterpoint. These facets of odor (of my odor, to be exact) continued to increase methodically, until they became almost deafening in my head. But the most significant thing, the clearest, lay in what those olfactory particles said to me (as if I cared): that I was alive, that I was alive!

In spite of this information, I couldn't move. The consciousness of my immobility was as strong as the certainty of my sense of smell. The fingers of my hands were absolutely rigid and the only sign of life in my extremities was an almost imperceptible movement from within that I thought came from my toes. On the other hand, I felt that the nerves transmitted those sensations to the brain with disproportionate slowness, as if time controlled the sensation as it does light from a distant planet. In any case, more than movement in the toes was the fact that blood circulated. And I set about examining with the greatest care all those other senses that I scarcely had. This made me think that little by little my extremities were thawing (after the thawing of the blood) and that a richer world of sensation was being created within the limitations of my putrefied person. I understood that the mere fact I thought about my frozen blood constituted an automatic acceptance of my previous death and that it was absurd to think I was alive if I accepted that possibility (unless I believed in the resurrection of the blood). Nevertheless, in spite of the inherent illogicality of my situation, I was coming to believe that the illogicality meant I was alive.

I don't know how much time went by until that same sensation of the blood's circulation took place in my hands. What's certain is that I expected it to happen, although I believed that I passed long hours, days perhaps, sleeping, breathing the odors in the depths of my subconscious. At some point, then, the blood began to circulate in my hands, and to my surprise I felt it in my legs, further than the knees, although my arms still remained rigid. In spite of these reviving sensations, I couldn't say whether I could move voluntarily or not.

I entertained myself, then, with the anticipation of movement that I was discovering in my body, although at times I grew bored and closed my eyes (as if I had them open) and slept (or believed I did). Perhaps it was all invention brought about by inactivity, but within that non-life I lived intensely, alternating between the excitement of the inexcitable and the extremes of the most profound depression. The periods of sleep were, then, a necessity to spare me the tedium and irritation of my bodily presence. And it was better thus, because after long periods of sleep I realized that I had made progress and that my condition was improving. The sensation of ice which had been so strong, disappeared gradually and I began to forget about it, as if I were changing into a mass of liquid that was not so cold. Nevertheless I still couldn't get away from the sense of persistent dampness.

(I really have little to tell about that period of my life— or of my death—and I'm afraid of boring the reader by prolonging it in this way, although I certainly don't want to omit anything that would distort the overall picture.)

The first auditory sensation reached me as a result of the sharpest pain, as if I'd been struck in the ear with a pick (of the kind they formerly used to split blocks of ice) or as if the ear had a suppurating wound that constantly secreted a green pus. The infection had possibly reached the eardrum. Obviously I couldn't see any of this, but when this sharp pain struck me unexpectedly (which produced a psychological pleasure), I thought I could see the whole process, as if a poison were running through my semicircular canals and causing dizziness. That pain, accompanied by an inexplicable loss of balance (that I couldn't lose since I was motionless) frightened me, but at the same time was further proof of life since it was a movement within the immobility. The pain in itself was very short but so sharp I wanted to cry out. At times I thought I placed my hands over my ears in order not to hear or feel it. The movement of my arms was pure supposition, although I recognized the inner impulse. I didn't know why I had that pain in my ears, but I firmly believed they were suppurating, and there were times I felt a kind of itching as if something moved along the auditory tract. Perhaps it was my blood, but I was tormented by the idea that larva had gotten in there and were moving through that labyrinth, disgusting me with the thought they might arrive in my mouth by way of the Eustachian tubes (which connected with the pharynx) and cause me to vomit. I knew that if that happened I was going to come out of my lethargy, since the spasms of nausea would move my whole body. Other times (when I had some sense of humor) I calmed myself by thinking I had something live in my ears and that that something wanted to talk with me and couldn't. Each time it tried it hurt me, without that communication (for a considerable time) changing into sound. At all events, there was a moment when for the briefest instant sound accompanied the pain which, because of its intensity, seemed to last an eternity. It was a sharp whistle, accompanied by a secretion (doubtlessly), that shot through my brain and made itself heard when it touched my eardrum. The strange thing was that when nothing happened (save in my olfactory subconscious), I began wanting that pain or sound and listened sharply in expectation of its return. It was company. The pain, however, was diminishing in intensity and was finally replaced by a persistent buzzing, as if I had an insect fluttering in those canals which, like the larva (but less disgustingly), wanted to be brought into contact with me. I hoped someday to hear a word that corresponded to these events.

Little by little, within my rigidity, I was obtaining a total consciousness of my body. It was everything such consciousness should be. I certainly didn't know if all my body were there. I might easily lack some part of it. It's true that if the same thing happens to everybody, even under normal circumstances, then how much more to me who was not at the moment precisely normal. Externally we know what's going on, but there is a group of organs

of which we have only a pictorial consciousness: the ad-
renal glands, the coeliac axis, the iliac artery, the urethral
orifice. They have to do with a series of conceptions whose
physical counterpart we are unacquainted with and might
easily be a representation of the artist, an imaginative
creation on the anatomic chart. It's clear that some internal organs have a definite reality for us: the beating of
the heart provides a consciousness of existence, the respiratory passages leave a vague sense of the flow of oxygen, the urine gives us a remote idea of kidney function.
In truth the digestive apparatus is one of the most con-
vincing since the route our dinner takes is a daily study
in change to which we are visual witness (at the beginning
and at the end): "by their works you will know them."
Naturally a detailed analysis is another matter, and there
is no certainty whatever that the version we are told might
not be part of the same fiction, this time literary. In any
case, it is not unusual that some of these unknown entities
we know by name (at times not even by name, since spe-
cialists and a few amateur scientists are the only persons
who have a relative familiarity with the psoas muscle or
the superior mesenteric vein, to mention simple examples,
since other times the use of Latin makes the existence of
the organ even more doubtful) fall prey to an infectious
disease, atrophy or, what is worse, some malignant tumor.
Since we live at the margins of such anonymous entities,
we aren't conscious of the dangers that menace us daily
save when the abstract image necessitates what we call
cure and they change into a painful reality that requires
treatment. Never before had I been so close to that sub-
world. It was a new experience, like living with the Mafia.
Although, as I have already indicated, I was not conscious
of each and every one of those elements that are frequently
mentioned as making up a person, the truth was that never
before in my life had I felt so near such possible knowl-

edge. These organs were my immediate company. Naturally I will not say I was in communication with the renal plexus—quite the contrary: I might easily lack one, cold as I was, without knowing it. Who can truthfully say that we *really* have a renal plexus? It was these fantasies (in the past) which had made me sick. What I was sure of in that moment was that "unknown materials" were inside that vague unity which seemed to be me: but I believed that of these "unknown materials" that I had or had had or was supposed to have, I might well lack some without my or anyone else's really knowing it.

This consciousness of the parts of my body must have taken place piecemeal, since I couldn't say that I realized my body was all one unit. In this way the idea that I was quartered wasn't long in occurring to me. A religious sentiment was intermixed with all of this, and although I had no consciousness of saintliness I considered the possibility that I was not a whole person but a partially putrefied heart preserved in a glass case. And a heart that, although it was completely uprooted from the body, still lived with the same rhythmic pulsations as always. The idea of being only a heart full of blood with the post-mortem beat of a lizard's tail parted from the body, seemed frightening to me. It was as if I were greatly afflicted, in great anguish. But I got the idea out of my head, believing that I was only a decomposed intestine—it was better to be that process of digestion, that disgust, than that blood. Anyway, I insisted on seeing myself as divided and in a crystal urn, and I sensed my half-putrefied finger with a ring and part of a fingernail was preserved at the foot of an altar.

I say I felt because I don't dare say I saw it. I insist consequently on affirming that everything was more felt than seen, although there are moments when the borders between one thing and another tend to become confused.

104

To see, what is called seeing, would be ultimate proof that I was going to recover, and although I had completely forgotten what pleasure was, whatever it was, I knew that it would come first. I want to make clear that when I anticipated nausea as a consequence of a possible worm in my mouth, I had no notion of pleasure but of disgust, and it was for this reason, I thought, that the nausea didn't become reality.

In any case, the absence of the sense of sight was in my opinion secondary to the absence of memory. I mean the presence of forgetfulness. In every instance when I was able to remember, I could imagine, see things; what happened was I couldn't always remember. The imagination can supply the absence of light, but first it has to exist in order to be able to imprint itself on the darkness. I can say that sight was therefore black, if it is possible to call sight not seeing.

At the same time that this concept was outlined in the darkness of my mind, another intangible was also taking shape. Lamentably it has to do with the memory of God. This explains that notion of bleeding remains that had evolved from what I was. The *I* which I had meant to create as a form of rot was still not created, although I am sure I no longer wished it since I had ceased to be, but it wasn't right that He should be and I still hadn't fulfilled my goal. In any case, it was not going to matter what I desired or ceased desiring, because the pre-existence of God laughed at an accomplished fact.

Nevertheless, I can't separate the imaginary act of seeing from the internal presence of God, since I needed to visualize Him as something specific (much as primitive man has done). The problem is that I didn't know, exactly, when I began peopling the black imaginings of my brain with illustrated memories. Abstractions of color were the first things I remember seeing (for sure). I couldn't remember faces, things, or myself. It is necessary to understand that the notion of oneself comes from the mirror and that although you can see many pieces of your own body, you can't see yourself except by means of reflections that man has invented. That is to say (under normal conditions) we see pieces of ourselves, but the body as a whole is a reflection. Especially we have no face and all the posterior part of our bodies (I'm not referring to the extremities) is absolutely unknown—at least under normal conditions and disregarding aberrations of the mind. We know these things by indirect references that others give us, by deduction on seeing the backsides of our supposed fellow creatures, by reading or through works of art with which we identify. Of all these versions of our being it is the mirror which offers the most objective. To yourself, you are no more than a reflection, the creation of a mirror, or a literary conception: I couldn't see myself, neither the parts nor the whole, and it is for this reason that the notion of myself was particularly remote.

The first thing I remember seeing (for sure) were abstractions of color. I couldn't remember faces, I couldn't remember things, but I began to see flat surfaces of color. I believe I passed whole days with some color. Possibly years. There were colors that I preferred, and I spent more time with them. Some colors were particularly difficult. Red was one of them, and I could only stand to look at it for a short space of time. Nevertheless, I liked to and I came to consider it a good exercise, since it shook me (within my immobility, you understand) and "made me advance." It had an irritating aspect which could be identified with the blood of bulls, but there was something mighty in that hue. The last to appear was luminous white, and it was so strong it blinded me and made me turn to my favorite color, which was, naturally, black. Not the black of sight, nor of blindness either. That is to say, at times I saw black and realized I was seeing it, but that it was my blindness. Other times I told myself I was going to see black, and then the sensation was different. It was a color that didn't cause fatigue because at bottom it was already dead.

Little by little I was able to make abstract squares, geometrical figures, spots of color. Totally flat, like primitive paintings lacking in depth. The whole pictorial process was removed, the lines taking the shape of what I now realize were people, but which I couldn't identify at that time. Obviously it was myself, but so schematic it could have been anybody. Finally, I began to remember things as painted, but badly, like the drawings of a child incapable of reproducing objects in the dimensional sense. In reality I don't believe I had the idea that things had dimension.

When I was in this stage, the concept of God took flat pictorial form. I was bothered (or I am bothered) by the fact He was seen before I, but that's the way it was. The first thing that I "saw" was a geometrical form, almond-shaped, in white, with a large round spot in the center. For a time I saw it (in quotes, naturally) as an abstraction of contrasting colors, but finally I realized it was an eye observing me. This eye, in reality, had no expression (since it was a primitive eye), but I came to realize it was implacable, irate, capable of cutting me in pieces without shedding a tear. I spent long periods in front of that almond-shaped figure. I don't remember the moment I realized it was the eye of God.

Little by little shades of color began to appear, irregular spots, and all at once I was illuminated by complete perceptions that were like tableaux. I believe it was then that I recovered my memory. Many times I saw completely lit rooms with people who never showed their faces. Naturally the faces were there, carefully painted, but I never saw them because I had never seen my own face. They were pictures without order or concert, like those in a museum. I believed that I was touring all the museums in the world and that I saw the most famous pictures, in every style, with the peculiar circumstance that I was the author of all of them. But I saw everything, remembered it, and forgot it by turns, so that in a certain sense it was as if I hadn't seen, forgotten, or remembered anything. Until the day I saw the geometric abstraction of that eye in a group of lines and circles that made another abstraction, but this time a complete one. At first I didn't realize that those lines were trying to represent something, and I allowed myself to be carried by the purely pictorial, although the presence of the eye (two of them, certainly) upset me, since I linked it to the eye which had looked at me with such insistence. But up to a point I had calmed myself, thinking it wasn't an eye but a geometric figure.

I don't know if it was the fact I spent such a long time looking at that reproduction that made me give it a concrete significance. From following the lines and colors so much, the shining surfaces, I realized that I was looking at the high part of an apse and that in that high part appeared God in all His majesty in the vesica piscis. Almost at the same time I saw the oval of a face and a body cut in two by a saw that was suspended by two matching eyes. About the figure there was nothing specific, except for a zigzagging red line that was the bleeding red line produced by the saw which divided the man in two. At the foot of this representation there was a figure lying inside a casket, and although its face did not show either, I was able to identify the man, and by extension myself. It wasn't hard to perceive the three levels of the building (that without doubt were the interior of a church), with God in His majesty on high in the apse, the body quartered in upright form on the altar, and inside the casket my recumbent body. Brightest of all was the terrible eye duplicated in the face of God, and since I didn't know my own I placed a pair like it in the body divided in two and another harmless pair in the recumbent figure, with the peculiarity that the God-like eyes ceased being terrible and became terrified. In any case, the (eye and) face of God in His majesty was pre-existent to mine and that concept mortified me because it turned me into a geometric reflection.

Whatever the truth of these incidents (which certainly were not precisely incidents), the first "visual" consciousness I had of myself (leaving aside that of the man being cut in two by a saw) was the image of my prone body. I had visited myself often, wearing a pilgrim's cowl (which hid me), and I grew to like this holy rhythm so much that I repeated the visits to the sanctuary from time to time, but carefully avoided the wound produced by the saw (that I couldn't stand for fear I might feel it), that and the frightful countenance of God in His majesty in the apse. As much as I enjoyed the duplicity of visiting myself, I didn't have clear control of the images (as if they were— and I was—both the picture and the fact) and many times the scene went on and I could no longer follow it, visualizing wholly at random. I was filled with anguish when my traveler didn't appear and days passed and he was nowhere to be found. Once I passed several weeks seeing fixed views of the court of Louis XIV, in Versailles, and I searched futilely among the courtesans, although I knew it was very doubtful that I was there. Since I couldn't see the faces I couldn't tell, but I knew that although I couldn't see myself, if I were there I would be able to recognize myself. The reason that I couldn't see faces was to avoid the possibility of reproducing the one that was geometrically known to me and which I feared. In any case, I passed a lot of time without seeing myself and it mortified me to be in that frivolous court where the men wore wigs and the women were always dancing the minuet. I couldn't do anything about it. When this happened it was necessary to ignore it and hope that something else would happen. It grew so that seeing so many views of that court tired me and I closed my eyes and slept, but sometimes to mortify me the visions came back in my sleep.

I don't recall the exact moment when I saw myself, this time seated before a typewriter. The fingers pressed the keys which jumped over the paper as if I wished to hurry the words, but produced lamentable errors rresor serror. Like the discarded pieces I remembered in the casket, I saw myself within a dream, but doubled now that I was putrefied in part while the other part wrote, or was I writing and the other part dreaming the putrefaction? Unfortunately for the reader, in that emptiness of my immobility in which I was nevertheless recovering the ability to think, anything was possible, as if I were a dream of myself writing about myself. This produced a terrible anguish in me that made me search for, or want to search for, a companion; but even more terrible was when I had that companion in the dream and I realized it was not a real companion but a nightmare. When I was afflicted in this manner, I wanted to die, and the sensation was more excruciating because I wasn't sure I still lived.

In spite of these passing tribulations, I felt relatively tranquil because I sensed that I was returning to something. So far as odors went, they were increasing and I realized that not only was I unthawing, but my clothes also, and it wouldn't be much longer until I was joined by the odors which had formed part of my reality. The essence of the overcoat, consequently, came like an advance warning of changes that were in the wind.

The full recognition of the presence of the overcoat around my body, offering warmth and the familiarity of its odors, had formed part of an intimacy, of a bond so tight that it is unnecessary for me to say much more about it. The relationship was so uniquely personal that it's like explaining the existence of an arm or a leg. There's no sense in it. I will limit myself to saying that I noted each odor-bearing particle of the overcoat and that each one produced a different memory. Such a phenomenon represented, purely and simply, my coming back to life.

I won't go so far as to say that I had the full presence of a returnee at that time, nor even the doubtful aspect of that other overcoat in the park, but it was clear I stood at the portals of re-entry. This awareness excited me inwardly, to the point where I could almost see myself. I wanted to outline my facial characteristics against the blackness of my closed eyes, but I couldn't get beyond those terrified, superimposed eyes that I didn't like. A consciousness of what was pleasing and displeasing continued to increase, and the tracks of pleasure and pain shone more brightly in my body. Evidently they made up the tactile senses. My body began to register the hard and the soft, the smooth and the rough.

Although I was immobile and couldn't touch myself, I felt covered with accumulated secretions. Sometimes I had the feeling my skin had turned scaly. At best they were the transparent scales of a fish. This idea seemed to be accompanied (or suggested) by the penetrating odor of fish split open and thrown one on top of the other in market showcases. But it had to do, I would say, with clean scales. Other times it was the oily idea of serpents' scales, a rancid penetrating odor, like an oil accumulated for years in a jar and beset by spoilage. There was no lack of even heavier sensations, and I felt myself being flattened as if the world pressed down on me, as if on top of my skin or becoming part of it, the crusts of accumulated dirt formed the thick scales of crocodiles, the protective carapaces of turtles, the iron shells of the crustaceans. I felt then that if that heavy mantle which covered me and was part of me could somehow be shed to become part of the earth's crust, I could find myself. Without warning, however, an entirely different idea might occur: my skin had turned so fine that I was transparent and I had the sensation that I was going to rip apart and that those invented organs would come spilling out, as if the skin vomited them through suppurating fissures. I then felt myself entirely covered by a grease that allowed me to slide this way and that and whose bland secretion formed a protective envelope. I was sunk in a doughy substance that swallowed me, covered me, and intruded even into my mouth.

One day, however, I had a more recognizable tactile sensation. It was outlined brightly, but with such simplicity it made me think I definitely wasn't dead. I realized I wasn't in a crystal casket at the foot of an altar, although my body was definitely prone. It was as if I were in an old bed with a worn-out mattress, hard and soft at the same time, including a few loose springs. These springs imprinted themselves in my flesh, and I especially felt one that probed my back with the penetrating consistency of a knife that didn't quite break the skin. This notion was lasting and had the character of a real discomfort, as opposed to the previous sensations that were too odd for me to be certain. The pain was fixed and never, after first feeling it, was I able to rid myself of it. At least not entirely. And the most important thing was that I didn't want to free myself from that pain because I knew that there in my back, at that point, the contact I was making with the outside world was far more real, or so I believed.

At the same time that I had a direct notion of pain, I began to get an opposing sense of something pleasant, or at least of something that wasn't so disagreeable, although

112

I will say that I wasn't particularly susceptible to anything enjoyable. In any case, I knew that certain parts of my body rested on surfaces that, if they weren't really fluffy, were at least somewhat soft. Also my fingers were receiving new sensations (not internal ones like the circulation of the blood, which by this time had become habit) but exterior ones. Sometimes I believed the contacts were rough, as if I touched old shriveled skin wrinkled by the years and the weather, others the sensation was smooth as if I touched the flat surface of a piece of paper. Attached as I was to these tactile sensations, I almost wished to hear them and tried to capture the tiniest sounds. Instead, an indistinct buzz that I never could hear clearly began to reach me from somewhere. It was, nevertheless, not the interior buzz of which I have spoken previously, but the exterior hum of diffuse conversation, some phrases very near my ear.

I can't deny that at this time I knew fear, almost panic. I was afraid of seeing, and at times I thought I could open my eyes, but for terror didn't. Nevertheless, I hadn't the least doubt that at some moment or other I was going to do it. During those intervals I didn't see anything for the simple reason that my eyes were closed.

A sensation that was both hard and soft, but undoubtedly pleasant, made me realize I had an erection. It was as if all the other feelings were annulled (in particular that pain in my back) and reduced themselves to that one sexual reality. It seemed that besides my heart, which had been preserved in the midst of the bleeding pain that was sealed in the glass urn, everything else I had been was nullified and there remained only the lone truth of a physiological circumstance. I had become, then, a truncated piece of biology, and the image imposed itself on my closed eyes. As soon as this happened, I saw the casket where I lay, stripped naked but rotten, everything except the part of my body where feeling had been concentrated. I glanced upward and saw myself, still divided by the saw which those two eyes had used to dismember me, my entire trunk split to the groin, where there was a long knife, destructive and painful, that was filling itself with pleasure. But to the degree that that pleasure rose toward the point of that blade, a bitter fluid ascended toward my throat, a nausea in the form of bile. The restored pleasure rose disgustingly toward my throat at the same time that that painful gratification descended toward the blade in my flesh. The conjunction of pain and pleasure took the form of the bloody semen of an orgasm that was produced in the black circle of that terrible almond-shaped eye.

I could hear, then, the distant rumor of a jubilant and joyous hosanna that came from the depths of the tabernacle. It was clear I was not alone (and I'm not referring to the alter egos present during my recent ejaculation, but to other creatures who approached in hurried flight). I was conscious and the attention of the chorus was inevitable. The hosanna which had resounded on the walls of the cathedral changed now into a hundred indecipherable screams. In spite of everything, I was not completely recovered. My awakening (which had taken place in the cosmic beats of my groin) had still not paid the full debt of my return.

It was for this reason that other images continued to beat inside my eyelids in proportion to the vigor of my recovered life. I would have to submerge myself in a fluttering nightmare in which my sexuality could find its own company. My progressive withdrawal had opened on an unknown exterior world (not only that singular almond-shaped eye) whose shrieks multiplied as if they came from birds, mythological birds in search of seeds. I felt them approach me hungrily, flapping and screaming, each time nearer so as to destroy all hope of sleep.

"Kkk Rrr Eee Www Fff Jjj Iii Aaa Zzz Xxx Ooo Ppp Ttt Ddd Eee Yyy Lll Bbb Ccc Fff Xxx Ooo Aaa Sss Jjj Uuu Ppp Mmm Rrr Yyy Eee Ddd Fff Lll Nnn Mmm Ddd Uuu . . ."

The voices screamed inside my head. They spoke, nevertheless. It was simply an agglomeration of dissonant sounds emitted by insects, birds, unknown animals. It was a language—sharp, penetrating, even, consistent—that I didn't understand at this time, but that, united with the other sensations, awoke me and aided in my resurrection.

"Kek Rar Eke Wew Fef Hij Iki Aja Zax Xix Olo Tit Pop Dad Ege Yty Lil Bab Coc Fef Xax Olu Aba Sas Joj Uju Igi Pip Mum Rir Yiy Eje Did Lol Non Min Don Udu . . ."

The voices were filling everything, beating one against the other, like the screaming of birds. They seemed to be enclosed in a crystal jar as if they wanted to join together to say something. It was as if a thousand migratory birds toured the heavens of my skull and directed themselves toward a warm rocky southland, pecking at its peaks with the voracity of hungry creatures of the air.

In the middle of this agony while flat on my back, a harmonious truth came over me: that what I was hearing was capable of being understood. Somehow I thought that the first step would be to embrace those sounds, and I convinced myself that that language would have a hidden meaning, not only animal, but to a certain extent human. I vaguely remembered the existence of certain famous scientists who had dedicated their lives to deciphering the language of certain animals, to the point where they understood them perfectly and constructed their own alphabet. With time I've realized that this absurd idea was purely an invention of my mind.

It was obvious that the barrier of ice which had separated me from the exterior world had disappeared and that this was the moment to communicate with something or someone. Although perhaps I didn't understand it all in that instant, what was happening to me was owing to a process of complete isolation that had begun (now I can say it) at the moment I chose the overcoat. This is to say that from time beyond remembering I was alone.

To return or not to return. I had to break the barrier that had been created both within and without, but I couldn't do it. I had no memory. That is to say, I couldn't remember exact experiences, persons with whom I had lived, but the consciousness that I had lived with someone in particular existed in part. But in the midst of my indecipherable depths did I want to return or did I want to stay? If I had known the unknown, I might have disappeared in that instant, but since I didn't know the final secret of my flesh and spirit I refused to pass beyond the blindness of my closed eyelids.

It was for this subconscious reason that I remained for a long time (and this is the most exact way of saying that I don't know whether it was hours, months, years) listening to those voices that had to have (I insisted) some meaning. Although all were the same, I adopted the custom of reconstructing them separately, thus creating the dialogue that sustained those unknown creatures.

"Kekuju Mumrir."

"Olotit Pepeje."

"Dududo Minaja."

"Zaziji Jojuju."

"Ekecoc Wewolo."

Perhaps I am boring the reader with a reconstruction of a language which he doesn't understand (nor did I at that time—or even later, as will be seen further on), but I have to do it to convey an exact sense of my character and situation. And it's not because this phonetic transcription has the least importance, since at bottom it is false. Nevertheless, in that falseness lies its significance: I was returning, but searched in that supposed communication for a reason not to. The tragedy of my situation (and I don't know if the tragedy lay in the possibility of my death or in the possibility of my revival) awoke in me a fictive interest in linguistic studies, which I had always specifically hated. I told myself (lying to myself) that if I allowed myself to be carried away emotionally by such things, I was going to knock down the walls that separated me from the surrounding world—and precisely for that reason I dedicated myself (possibly because of an immense cowardice) to doing the exact opposite. Wasn't it these walls which had separated me from everything and confined me under the strange circumstances in which I now found myself? Why not begin learning the language of those strange creatures (probably birds) with which I was living in such a strange manner? Wasn't this the best way to understand my "fellow creatures"?

I believe that I really did try to convince myself. And, nevertheless, how mistaken I was! How could I fool myself again? What an intense desire not to return, to bury myself in the overcoat, in the snow, in those immense blocks of ice where I had frozen! The horror of isolation was as intense as the dread of company! But I didn't even have the courage to tell the truth about what was happening to me—truth that, after all, I didn't know.

How far from the mark were the arbitrary reconstructions of those sounds that I easily could have done in a completely different manner! The creation of words was the first step that I proposed to myself, but instead of creating the words of others, I set myself to creating my own. Since all the sounds were identical in their tones and since they lacked inflection—there had been a complete absence of shading—possibly I was uniting in one word a harmonious output which was the product of many

117

creatures. The sameness of the voices made it impossible to separate individuals, and in reality the only individualized process was my own. I was trying to individualize the screams of a band of birds, isolating them one from the other in order to make words out of them. The task was impossible and as such a mask for my own fear. Fear that was double, for I was as much afraid of leaving my present condition as I was of remaining in it. At all events, I prolonged those phonetic investigations inside my head and found an unexpected pleasure in doing so. In this way I was creating my own dictionary and pursuing repeatedly the same syllabic combinations until I could be really certain of them. I understand that the process (seen now from a distance and in light of other more advanced linguistic studies) was absolutely unscientific and answered a psychological need. Although I hadn't the least basis for rejecting one possibility and adopting another, I did so anyway, perhaps to prolong the process of evasion. The moment had to arrive when a decision had to be made between all these forms. I became convinced that Elecoc Wewolo meant something, although I could just as easily have formed the words Cocele Olowew. If I heard Zazele Ijlicoc Wewujo Jojolo, I decided to put those sounds in the order of my own creation and insisted that Zaziji Jojuju Elecoc Wewolo was what had been said. This indicates, simply, that my supposed longing to communicate isolated me and that at bottom I was acting in accord with my personal desire not to communicate. I preferred to invent in my own way, creating my own language by means of an arbitrary interpretation of theirs. Today it seems to me it has always been that way and that in every word there exists the residuum of our own sonorous interpretation and that that subconscious interpretation is opposed to the general one and makes true communication impossible. The words of a language have been

118

imposed on us, and it is for this reason that we never have the exact same understanding of the things about us—but in reality these theories (no doubt curious but with little scientific basis) ought not to distract the reader from the things that were happening to me at that time.

Since I was deceiving myself, I could go back and reconstruct what I had invented. Nevertheless, the moment came when I thought I'd covered all the phonetic possibilities and I would be obliged to decide in favor of one of the verbal irrealities I myself had created.

Whatever phonetic reconstruction I might make, the truth was it hadn't the least meaning for me, while before me lay the equally arduous task of making sense of the things I'd invented. How would I be able to translate that unknown language that I, in numberless false transcriptions, had created? Besides, did that identical interrupted scream have any meaning? I insist on pointing out the most absolute absence of tones and shades. At times it was not even an animal sound: it could easily be the whistle of a boat blowing in the inner chambers of my hearing. In any case, however it was, I had to give it some significance. The solution was going to be very simple since I was going to designate a content with the same arbitrary authority that had guided me in determining the form. Although in the reconstruction of the sounds I had some material basis for my doubtful conclusions, in assigning them concrete significance I could only resort to my own invention. Still (I clearly remember this) I was not disposed to accept what I heard as untrue or the meanings that I gave it as false. Consequently, all the dialogue of those birds (a conclusion at which I had already arrived and which we will see is true—at least in part) is completely in keeping with the truth.

The first step lay in discovering some intention in those screams, and after some time passed and I hadn't been able to I finally detected (I don't know how) an obscene purpose. This certainty was determinative of the way I translated the words. Yes, in the interior of that uniform scream I was able to distinguish most clearly (in the midst of its filth) a brothel sordidness. I was sure (I told myself) that beaks produced those sounds, the beaks of birds, some crooked, some straight, some of them flattened, deformed perhaps, all beaks foulmouthed and dirty, but feminine and stimulating; round open mouths, at times curved, thick lips classically fleshy, with a voluptuous red tongue, damp, disposed always toward suction. Thus the phonetic organ surged in my consciousness with a duplicity that was not contradictory for me, but complemented the double function of woman and bird.

What were those creatures whose open beaks produced those screams whose significance was beyond me unless I could confine them within the frontiers of the human? Perhaps they had to do with a vanished mythological species whose realm I had entered. Was I the creature elected to be their medium? Obscene laughter rose in the midst of that continuous and singular screaming. I couldn't say if it was a hundred birds or a hundred women, and I thought it might be a creation of my mind, which would disappear completely, once and for all, if I dared to open my eyes. But I wouldn't do it, besieged naturally by fear. My passion to confirm a truth didn't reach that far. It was then the words I translated were spoken with a sarcasm that made the erection of my body bleed. They were, yes, mythological birds, indecent and whorish, that emptied into my ears the piercing obscenities I wished to hear. Those twisted beaks that I still hadn't seen opened themselves in those round exclamations that kissed me and joined themselves to my mouth. The same gross way that voices beat against one in a brothel, so did the sensation that came back to me, consuming me in a neatly curved,

120

voluptuous extravagance. The forms writhed in a sordid eternity of pleasure.

Soon I was able to repeat everything they had said since those first screams, which may have risen in unison although I heard them separately.

"Okele cha ki naiii?"

("And he was almost dead?")

The expression had produced strident guffaws and someone had added:

"Wewano Jolomobu."

("The flesh resurrected.")

The funny riposte produced new gales of laughter. I thought that they were referring to me and to the contrast between their state of dress and my shameful nudity. Because I didn't have the least doubt that I was naked, and I felt my hands run confusedly over some wounds produced by some webbed feet; a vulgar hairy chafing ran over me in all directions, plus an intense feathered fluttering in the area of my testicles, as if some birds were competing furiously for food that was necessary for them and would be found in that location. I returned to my senses in the middle of that nightmare.

I am not going to subject the reader to the tiring process of having to listen to the story in two languages, since bilingualism is not one of the fundamental intentions of this work. I only wish to point out that the raw animal insolence was much more marked in the scream that was produced in the original language, perhaps because of, what might be called in modern linguistic terminology, the plane of emphasis. This plane of emphasis is the tone used by mythological birds during the mating season, to which Homer refers so cleverly in his tale of the sirens. The reader will imagine the grave peril in which I found myself! Consequently, it is not only prudent, but necessary (according to the rules of good speech and because of the

121

consequences to which evil talk might carry us) that I tell all (or almost all) in my own language.

"Swallow it, dog . . . !"

"There's a lot to suck up!"

"Wait for them to smear you with ointment."

"Blow."

"There it goes."

I ought to add that the voices (if so they may be called) are all part of a series of experiences that took place in unison. Soon all my senses had awakened, integrated nevertheless in that one. I had a terrible fear, as if I were going to be the victim of an absolute disembowelment by the birds. It was not that I feared (as in that mural I had seen somewhere) lying on a barren plain at night with buzzards feeding on my remains. I was lying in a wilderness, that was true, and the birds were pecking tirelessly at a regrettable erection, feeding on it, but without making it go away. I had the full sense I wasn't frozen and thus it appeared that a little thread of semen ran over me continually, as if it were part of an open wound in a point of rock—a white river coming from my being. I felt the wingbeats of those birds which I still hadn't even seen (but had wrong-headedly visualized in my mind), and I looked forward with terror to the moment we should meet.

"Even your grandfather?"

"There was no help for it . . ."

"Bad night . . ."

"Pretty mistress . . ."

If the sound and supposed tone of those screams were hurtful, it was natural that the translation I imagined must be shameless, dirty, obscene, and cruel. It is for this reason I have decided to pass right over some of them and to retain only those that have appeared to me less wounding. I wish to note, however, that the language dealt with

122

the defilement that those hundreds of intruding webbed feet with sharpened nails constantly produced, in their incessant exploration, on my naked skin. I felt literally covered with wings, and their plumage was a kind of relief that contrasted with the superficial wounds produced by their claws and beaks.

"Neither more nor less . . ."

"What a beak of gold!"

"To rise and fall!"

"How many stairs!"

"Who would believe it!"

The time came when my understanding of the language was such that I stopped translating and simply thought in it, arriving at an immediate and automatic understanding of their words. This naturally increased the ecstacy that was born in me with the voices. How delicious to allow oneself to be carried by that deafening feminine gabble of stabbing claws that came from those hundred sucking beaks and those web-footed limbs! Never before had I imagined a similar pleasure. The screams were speaking at the same time and the words struck against each other in the air and fell on my body in voracious bites.

"And he was almost dead!"

"From quiet waters . . ."

"Are they hot?"

"What about the other one!"

"A cold that burns."

"I'm available!"

"How it throws off sparks!"

How strange it had all been! The initial irritation had transformed itself into a morbid sensual pleasure. Everything had begun with those metallic statements which had given way to a nervous excitation that changed me and wouldn't let me close my eyes (that I had closed) and rest.

I had felt bothered and irritated (and I still felt that way).
I had decided on an activity that I considered strictly intellectual, but in the midst of it the annoyance and discomfort had increased along with the pleasure. This explains the delightful concentration that I had experienced
on hearing that language and a charm that ran somewhere
between the erotic and the intellectual that each word
produced in me (especially if I didn't understand it), and
as each nonexistent nuance sharpened my instincts. Could
one say that it all had to do with the monotonous beat
of drums in whose mechanical repetition lay the elemental
emptiness of a repeated friction? Enthusiastic, they
couldn't do more than pick at me with their cries.

"The same dog!"
"What an experiment!"
"The force of destiny."
"Run or he'll bite you!"
"What a fate!"

I had the sense I was in a hermetically sealed room. If
that was true or not, I still didn't know, for I hadn't opened
my eyes. I had come to the conclusion that my blindness
increased the pleasure, and that acted as a sensory excuse
not to open them. I was able to recognize that peculiar
sensation one feels when he enters a room without the
least current of air and where the same odors have remained stagnant for a long time, as if they wished to
preserve their swampy purity. It is for this reason that that
place, whatever it was, was impregnated with a strong
odor that was like air (worn out or perfumed, it depends)
that almost asphyxiates and that shortened my respiration
and made it spasmodic. I insist that I was besieged by a
multitude of sensations that seemed to strike one against
the other and that these sensations pursued me to build
on each other. What is odd is that my panting respiration,
in consequence of that damp collection of odors, instead

124

of bothering me formed part of the absolute pleasure that was invading me. The sharpest and most penetrating scream irritated me but at the same time ran through me sensually in such a way as to produce an agreeable tension in all the tissues of my body. The secret of it all lay in the sensory contradiction that I was living. At the same time that I felt hermetically enclosed, I had the sensation that I found myself in wide-open country breathing to the bottom of my lungs that stabbing freshness of an orgasm that was both feminine and animal and was changed into air. But this countryside, in the last instance, was closed, hermetically, as if they had put it in a room, large but also hermetically sealed.

"Run or he'll bite you!"

"He's not chained."

"I thought not!"

"You were right."

"What a rich baby pacifier!"

"It teaches everything."

"We've learned a lot here."

I remained with my eyes closed in order that certain faculties—auditory, olfactory, tactile—might sharpen themselves even more. From an absolute absence of sensations I had passed to a multiplicity of them. A change had been produced, not in the appearance of things, but in my spiritual attitude and physical remains. I couldn't see myself and I didn't wish to, but now I knew. Not in vain had I suffered a terrible anguish, and I didn't want to go back to that desperate emptiness. Now all that covered me was a rough, crude surface that fossilized me in another way. I was a monument that raised itself over the grave of myself, and every contact evoked in me a life which had been lost since time immemorial—continents submerged in the depths of the waters. My entire body lifted itself with the voluptuosity of a stone made flesh in spite of its petrified unfeeling appearance.

"As soon as he heard the conga."

"Everyone revived."

"Life everlasting."

"Kettle drums sound."

"The flesh that consumes itself in fire."

"Here is the oven that burns."

"What a strong stomach!"

"He likes the pepper."

Was it really I that revived? And who was I? Over me I felt the fluttering of those creatures that woke me and had sewn throughout my body a unique desire that was at the same time an aberration of my spirit and flesh. Who were those beings? I told myself they had to do with some vanished mythological species, that I was dead and had entered another kingdom, but at the same time that level of sensation in contrast to its absence which I had experienced until recently told me that I was more alive than before. Was it perhaps that I had turned into a mythological species myself, a vertical idol of stone capable of experiencing pleasure on being loved? Perhaps I was the sensibility of the rock? They appeared to know everything and did nothing more than scream impudently at my immodest nakedness.

"He's a past master."

"A notable masseuse."

"What wisdom!"

"Rise and go forth!"

"To revive a dead man!"

"Supine stability . . ."

The dual sensation ran all through me. ("Better to rest wekolo kue leave us.") At the same time I felt that fluttering of birds over my body ("Lane was I murine lua quite sure"), the smooth downiness and intimacies of

126

some open lips ("The faith ojuako that dulequet sustains us"), glossy and feminine ("The gum danolo compresses gu"), is carried over my flesh ("life non putrefied is"), covering with its sticky humidity the lesions that were produced by their web-footed steps. ("I understand the indirect oke.") That sexual humidity was a voluptuous balsam over the wounds caused by those cloven hooves ("Note rewtui the oti verdict du"), and the delight that grew out of that contact compensating the smarting caused by those curved ("Caliente hot teacher porfesuc") corneas. So I felt, at the same time the stabbing but delicious lacerations of the footsteps ("Iqui iqui iqui iqui iqui!") that had nestled in my flesh, the smooth and downy friction ("Instruct durtac the ignorant") of some pelvises that visited me and that cured with the balsam of their organic humidity the wounds they themselves had ("To climb the mountain") occasioned ("To go down to the river bank"). Because they were desperate birds that rose and fell, searching blindly in their primitive descents ("Wakolo so! Wakolo so!") the hallucinatory satisfaction of their own ("I suppose they've already found him!") sex. Meanwhile some drag themselves ("osuko") over my skin ("osuko mi") and others penetrate me with their nails ("garras"), some take off and ascend ("upu") to leave room for new forms to seek sustenance ("fukun") that I gave them. They were dominated by a voracious hunger ("The flesh ab urbe condita resurrecta") and fought with one another ("The ass ad vitam strokes aeternum the ass") through that contact which was necessarily ("Deviris") mine. If before all feeling had disappeared ("Nessum maggior dolore che ricordarsi del tempo felice nella miseria"), now they came back over me and struck me, as if it were part of a sensory baroque. Everything appeared full of forms to me ("He contends udi kill the pistol"), and the forms became rough like the waves, all gilt. It was as if

I had the stability of an altar ("In naturabilus") and as if each revolution followed by the tips of my fingers ("Ay, how rich to touch!") ended in a desperate, twisted, feminine movement ("Wahine opertu"), union of bodies ("singular") in a form both hard and soft ("to sail a ship on a determined course!") at the same time. The beaks search ("The work ferbet boils opus") avidly for seeds in my body, in the depths of my testicles, as if in my system lay the germ ("grano") of their own harvest. I had ceased being ("Quis, quid, ubi, quibus auxilis, cur, quomodo, quando") to change myself into a pagan structure fertilized by birds.

I was rigid on the bed, incapable of moving under the mantle of those creatures that covered me. I felt them sheltering me with their body heat as if it were the middle of winter and the room had become superheated by the oily vapor of their bodies and mine. I sweated copiously and felt the stickiness of that flesh and those wings.

They were heads with wings. The wings grew out of their ears. Their black lustrous feathers opened themselves above me like the fans of bats. Blind, they flew confusedly because their eyes were gouged out and the sockets were empty. They were guided by the strong scent they gave off, bumping into one another as they searched uncertainly for places to land. Attracted by the exhalations of my flesh, they found me and fought frenetically for possession of every inch of ground on my body, growing still more excited. Their endless round mouths opened with their thick sucking lips that sometimes turned into beaks, now straight, now curved, but disposed to wound and to heal with the sticky saliva of their horn-like fleshy kisses. Of their bodies, besides their web-footed extremities ending in the small sharpened claws already mentioned many times, all that existed were the parts essential to sex. Some long flaccid breasts, at times longer than their limbs, hung downward, sweeping me with the tips of a thousand tired nipples, appendages without life and deprived of enchantment, bare shadows of something that must once have been beautiful. Common to all of them was a dense hairiness such as covers an open pubis in persistent orgasm.

CHAPTER
6

When I opened my eyes, I seemed to hear the wing beats of birds going out by the window. However, I couldn't see anything because the room was completely in darkness (unless I was blindfolded), and although my eyes looked out at darkness it was my own and not that of a conventional room which was strange to me. Besides, my brain was sluggish and at the same time aglow with those images which had filled it for some while. It wasn't possible that the birds had gone out by the window, for there didn't appear to be any, and had such existed they would have been closed. In the face of such contradictions I thought that all *that* must have been a febrile product of my imagination, and I remembered the sentence (in a legal sense) which read as follows: "When reason sleeps, monsters appear." I repeated it many times mentally, as if the fact I was awake protected me from those monstrous visions. I must not sleep again.

I had the sense that someone was taking my pulse and that others kept watch over my blood, while still others spied on my temperature. Scientifically organized, this synthesis of my life appeared on a screen in the form of an irregular line. It was relatively stable and for the first time in a long time (years perhaps) I had a feeling of relaxation (although momentary) that was almost un- known to me. But how long was it going to last? I thought that I had invented all those birds and all that frozen state which I had experienced and that in the last instance had come to nothing. If such had been the case, the thing was to find out at what point I had begun to invent *everything*.

What added to my certainty was the evident return of my memory, because I remembered many things that I believed were lost forever. It bothered me, of course, that many of these recollections were of irrational moments, but on taking an objective view, on looking at them from a reasonable angle, the certainty I had imagined every- thing only grew. I told myself that everything, absolutely everything, would have a logical explanation.

I felt, then, the moist contact of a sponge over my entire body, that I was resting on a soft enveloping surface that produced that refreshing effect of comfort and (I couldn't avoid an imperceptible shiver) of cleanliness. I had re- turned to a state of nature, immersed in that bath of quietude of the recently born (after the hecatomb of par- turition, I thought, again contradicting myself). I came out of that previous stronghold swimming in a capsule of water, breathing rhythmically in a dream of forgetful- ness. I floated in an undersea world, submerged in images of algae and of fish that slid through a musical, almost symphonic, silence as though it were a bath of God. After- wards my mother (whom I had forgotten) bathed me, submerging me in a baptismal font. I was naked but in a state of total purity, free of sin of whatever kind that lay without.

At the bottom of that sea, the sponge slid smoothly over my skin, which turned smooth as it lost blue-black particles, bits of tissue, dead dry cells, scales of a past which floated around me, scattering themselves in that hygienic, mythic, and sacred bath. They were blue-black

131

particles that floated off as if bidding me adieu, in a solitary disengagement of what had been, paining me (I couldn't help it) with their departure. Because they *were* I. I detected signs of malice in them, perhaps the crafty attitude of malignant cells that are extirpated and do not fulfill their destiny. The tissues of my body, organic and inorganic, joined with the dead cells of the overcoat, and all fell away as if the cold had been a burn. I cut short the image by turning my head, frightened by the optimism and anguish of that terrible rending.

I began to remember in less grandiloquent terms; that is to say, like any other man jack. That unhealthy pomposity of my first memory could do me no good and could lead to a return of recent bad habits. My brain was filling with reasonable memories: my parents, my infancy in a country town, the school I had attended, the shift of my family to the capital, my university studies: little things with greater significance. Perhaps it was time to bring a little sense to the sudden switches in my life, to provide the facts that fit the situation. Because, after all, I had to be (besides) the product of something, the result of specific events (real ones) that formed my identity. But in direct proportion as these things came to mind (because I really did remember) I erased them, tearing the sheets of paper where I had recounted the deeds of my life. I realized they didn't have the least importance (neither my given name nor my surname), and as such formed superfluous material. I saw myself as someone who contemplates an album of photographs (that boy who took his first communion) or as if I looked at a stranger. Only the marrow made sense, if indeed there were such a thing. But at all events, the process of being able to remember myself concretely, forgetting afterwards if I so wished, was a clear indication that I had recovered my mental faculties and was able to establish a continuity that would carry me by measured steps, and with all their usual details, to the happy shedding of the overcoat.

Among other things, I remembered my juvenile ambitions of becoming a writer, with all the attendant fanfare of words, my first meeting with Amanda and the crumbling of the ground as an island came to pieces under my feet. Everything came back, but in so natural a way that it seemed absurd for it to return in this manner, to the point that I felt a certain inquietude. How was it possible that my brain could change its way of seeing things so abruptly, when until recently all had been part of a crazy dream? It made no sense. From a world in which I had seen myself surrounded by strange creatures (which I could still reproduce with relative ease on my retina) I had returned to the simple realities I remembered so well.

There were two things which told in the back of my mind, two facts which seemed more important to me than the others: my marriage with Amanda and my desire to write. I remembered also how those two commitments were connected to the two symbolic losses which had taken place when we left the country: the loss of the wedding dress and the loss of my typewriter. I wanted to reject the idea, but I couldn't. I told myself that to succumb to the temptation of giving symbolic significance to simple events which were related only to the political mechanics of the country (those two items had been confiscated as a result of routine bureaucratic policy) was to fall into a trap. How was it possible that an adult like myself (and of at least average intelligence) could let himself be carried away by such foolishness? I should put an end to ideas of this sort, buy myself a Remington or an Underwood, and sit myself down to write a novel; and, to rid myself of doubts and to remain tranquil forever, buy Amanda a wedding dress, or perhaps with an eye to practicality, a white gown.

This kind of reasoning calmed me, but some things remained slightly unsettling. I refer to the overcoat. ("To the overcoats, you mean," and I almost seemed to hear Amanda's voice.) It was evident (I remembered this simply and fully) that after acquiring the overcoats our lives took a surprising spin and our behavior became rather strange. To remember things related to the overcoat bothered and upset me, in particular because I couldn't find a logical explanation for them. (And now, naturally, I had become very fond of logic.) I tried to make a summary of what had happened and told myself that the overcoat ("The overcoats, you mean," Amanda repeated with a brightness that surprised me and that gave the impression that she was here) had been another symbolic representation (a little like a novel, I said, to calm myself), of a kind of psychological abyss that had been created between us and that acted as a barrier trying to separate us (and it might have succeeded). But I tried to put aside such imaginings that didn't appear very healthful to me. After all, it was absolutely natural that marriages should suffer one crisis or another, and if ours was reduced to the question of the overcoat ("Of the overcoats, you mean," she repeated), it was a pretty small thing.

Consequently, with a very fine logic (although a little novelesque, much to my regret), the matter was reduced to three objects which in the last instance had little importance: a wedding dress, a typewriter, and an overcoat ("Some overcoats, you mean," she said, without understanding that I gave more importance to mine because hers, after all, had fit her rather well and had helped her— or so I thought—to find work). Although I feared to go again to the Hills of Ubeda (an abstract expression) and make a tour of the business (what happened before), I told myself that the simplest thing would be to get rid of the overcoat ("Of the overcoats, you mean," she added, but now I didn't pay her a bit of attention). Yes, I had to rise and get rid of the overcoat as quickly as possible.

As quickly as possible? In this simple and logical decision I had to confront an unexpected difficulty, which I tried to make a matter of humor, although it afforded me none. I couldn't move. I couldn't get up. I couldn't avoid the fact that this displeased me greatly, since I thought (with very good sense) that my immobility ruined my logic. I tried to take the matter lightly and thought that I had never been a lover of sports and that perhaps my lack of exercise was linked to these excessive imaginings to which I was prone. Undoubtedly a failure to exercise had hurt me always, and now I saw myself obliged to pay the price. The old saying *mens sana in corpore sano* came to mind, although not to my body, and I mightily regretted never having been a lover of handball, swimming, basketball, weight lifting or any of those other things invented by the English. I made a firm resolution to change the rhythm of my life in the future—if I ever succeeded in moving and leaving this quagmire.

The plan to escape "at top speed" came back like a dart aimed at the target of my consciousness, increasing my state of confusion. Because, what was my goal? And, what was even more incomprehensible, what was my point of departure? From where to where? Because to know, to know exactly where I was was something I still didn't know—and how many things had happened was something I might never know. My negative attitude toward external reality had put me in a blind alley. For this reason I "moved" by feel. The possibility of . . . escaping seemed more than doubtful. I had recovered my sense of feel but couldn't move so as to make use of it. Apparently I had a head, a trunk, and limbs (with all the accessories that go with them), but very limited possibilities (for the moment) to make effective use of such instruments. It was

135

as though I were made out of . . . stone (or ashes). "Bad news this," I told myself. The very fact I chose a literary image (being made of stone), that I conceived of that physical metaphor, was negative, even more if I added—who knows if it was to stymie my efforts?—the afterthought of "ashes," which had no foundation whatever. These "reasonings" unsettled me. At this point I was so tired of myself that I didn't know when in hell I was going to return to that normal life that others lived (or so I believed, right?), that everyone ought to live—or almost everyone. Maybe I was undernourished, ill-fed, lacking in vitamins, sick in some very real way that had nothing to do with the fantastic and that explained why I didn't have strength to move. I remembered that in times past (before the—"supposed"—freezing) I had hardly swallowed a piece of bread all day, accompanied at the best times by a cup of coffee. Therefore, it was completely natural that I should find myself in that state of absolute prostration. Since I was in the best of mental health, as soon as Amanda . . . returned . . . from her work, I would explain everything to her and between the . . . two of us . . . we would seek some . . . solution.

At the same time these thoughts were going through my head, I realized my ideas were not consistent, and my arguments seemed to stutter as I went on developing them. Amanda's absence was evident, and I had to confront the doubtfulness of her return . . . In order to return, Amanda had to have been here before, and if I didn't even know where I was what guarantee had I that she did? From here the supposed "solution" went contrary to all logic. If Amanda were unable to return because she had never been here, which was the major premise; there would be no encounter, which was the minor premise; and consequently no solution—a conclusion at which I was forced to arrive and the pure negation of all solutions.

With such a simple point of view I deducted that, at least, I wasn't crazy. It had to be something physical which had carried me to that state of prostration, and perhaps I would have to take some tonic or, at the most and in our best tradition, one of those chicken soups that raise the dead, in which case they wouldn't have to . . . hospitalize me.

The last word was like a slap in the face. So that was it. Crazy, frozen or sick—for whichever of these reasons— my condition had grown so critical I'd had to go to one of those horrible box-shaped city hospitals, masses of gray or reddish bricks where one joined a list of missing persons. At this point I remembered the dark accounts I had heard from some of my paralyzed countrymen and feared that I'd fallen in the same trap. But perhaps I was some miserable tramp without even a place to fall dead, who had finally found shelter and food in a well-regulated cell. My frightened heart skipped a beat; it was a sad octopus that palpitated inside the cavern of my chest, a piece of machinery that regularly expelled (thank God!) its submarine tint. The sponge of the nurse who was bathing me went on eliminating my uncleanliness systematically, which gave the room an atmosphere of air devoid of oxygen. Smoothly, almost delicately, she was little by little removing the filaments of the overcoat, the textile matter of my physical covering. Long filaments of my skin were detached with it, interwoven with the 80% wool and the 20% polyester. The skin that showed here and there had a delicate smoothness and a new sensitivity to pain, innocent, as though it were the naked layer of a burn you have forgotten as it healed over.

"The danger has passed now," the doctor said, smiling and looking at me fixedly.

The fear of being dead terrified me (although it should have calmed me) and I remembered the words of Joan

Woodward after her hysterectomy (in a scene that matched a recurring image of my own): "How is it possible I am still alive?" Because only death (and here I hoped that I was wrong) could confirm that all our dangers were past.

"You should get these ideas out of your head," insisted the doctor, as if my head were transparent and he was reading my thoughts, "for they do nothing more than upset you. You have to do your part. It's the only thing that stands between you and getting well."

I had lived, in truth—he was not going to deny it—through very dangerous circumstances, traveling the slothful paths of my thickening blood. And nevertheless my own body chemistry had reacted. But now I had to do my part to re-establish myself completely (almost). If I fixed my eyes on the rearview mirror, he told me, I might have an accident, because that way I wouldn't know what lay ahead.

I listened with attention, although I looked at him with incredulity, as if that man who had undertaken to confirm my vital signs was lying to me. But why would he do such a thing? What motive could he have? What was there to gain? The "parable of the rearview mirror" had all the earmarks of absolute truth, the two and two make four of a syllogism that I never had been able to understand. It was at once a basic scientific equation and an elemental medical prescription. And nevertheless it was as difficult for me to follow as those evangelical principles which ask us to deny ourselves. It was for this reason that, in spite of everything, I fixed my glance on the rearview mirror and the image came back of myself wrapped in the overcoat. I felt myself falling from the edge of an abyss into a whirlpool without beginning or end. It was a dizziness that erased everything. Hypnotized by the rearview mirror, my inner eyelids fell. With foot on the accelerator, I caused myself to descend frenetically along the spiral road that circled a volcanic mountain bordered by cliffs. It was the final "suspense" of a motion picture, the overcoat looking at me from behind, distracting my eyes from all that lay ahead: the road signs that marked the dangerous curves, the line in the asphalt, the lights of the cars that came from the opposite direction. My glance was fixed on the past as if I could only see myself as what I had been. Wrapped in the overcoat, listening to a distant echo that called to me, the siren song of my own voice, my being in my throat—what I was, what I had been, the entire past denying the future that still remained to me and that I had to forge with a will of iron. I knew that it was essential to cut, to break the image of the rearview, to see the new physiognomy of my being: I knew that this was the only way to save myself. But how? In what way? By what means?

I have to thank God that I'm still alive, because many people under similar circumstances have not been so lucky. This argument seems to me not only reasonable, but overwhelming, frankly incontrovertible; and yet there comes from below this saying from the devil's scrapbook: "That another's bad luck is a fool's consolation." A narrow escape frightens us no more than it frightens flies, which will always return with their notorious impertinence. That is to say, through a process of "thank you, God," one could resolve everything, peace on earth and glory in heaven. But it's too easy . . . and too difficult. It was not that I might have preferred death. I was bound to life, not only like every other mother's son, but possibly with greater intensity, although not necessarily with more effective means. I sought a harbor of salvation wherever it was. Whatever would keep me from going under. Quite simply, I wished to live. And it was then I attempted a "hallelujah," but my voice failed; it turned hoarse, ceased almost altogether, as if my throat had turned dry.

In this way, my "mistrust of God" (which was nothing less than what I felt for the doctor), snatched me brutally away from any possibility of absolute humility, and so became my sin. To believe was the most difficult. Because I couldn't stop thinking that I was in a trap, that I lived in a "suspense" so total it surpassed even the limits of a film by Hitchcock—much more so if it was true that I was hospitalized. Life (that is to say, death) was much more intense than Janet Leigh knifed in the bathtub, or in whatever place, by a second-rate lunatic. I did not know at what moment, in what unexpected instant, the crime would take place and the dead man, who had walked away from the previous scene, from that warehouse of clothed corpses, would end as he did in all the realistic movies (more certainly than in Hollywood in its happiest years), where there never was a "happy ending."

In short, it was most important, I repeated to myself time and again, to avoid a relapse at all costs, because the danger of the overcoat (which meant freezing, absolute paralysis, and being totally undone), had been beaten (although this was no guarantee that it might not return). This awful ambivalence irritated me, put me in a bad humor (inwardly), because what I wanted was an absolute affirmation or negation, a definite truth (or a lie)—which in the last analysis no one gave in that cursed hospital (assuming it was a hospital and not an asylum or a church), where information was withheld from me at every turn.

Why couldn't I stop tormenting myself? Perhaps it was enough to know that I had thawed out, had been skinned, and was more or less warm? That my heart continued beating, my lungs breathing, my kidneys producing urine and that my stomach and intestines continued making

140

sewage? Wasn't I still functioning? And if someone sneaked up and asked me, wasn't it true that I could still enjoy an orgasm from time to time? Then what? Where did the blight come from, that touch of the violin, that tango lament? Shit, from nowhere! I was my worst enemy and only by a surgical procedure, decisive and radical, could I extirpate that sickness from my disastrously confused past and perform, I myself with my lancet, a trepanation of the skull.

But, how about the overcoat?

It was true, the doctor told me, I had still not gotten rid of it entirely, because it had incrusted my skin for so long that it had turned into a configuration of myself, to the point of putting down roots. "A serious case, certainly, but not incurable." The symbiosis had been stubborn and far-reaching, as if someone had sewn it to my flesh, a kind of metallic chasing done with surprising skill. Or in the manner of a tattoo. It had adhered in such a way that it had already begun to attack my internal organs, impairing their function. In some places it was hard to tell where the superimposed matter began, whether woolly or industrial particles of a chemical nature, and where my own body ended, making the intervention of a surgeon imperative. Subjected to such influence, all my functions had atrophied, as if an excess of grease produced by the weavings of the overcoat, on being assimilated by the blood, had stultified the circulatory system and hardened the arteries. Because of all these clinical factors, the accumulated fat in my body had increased in marked disproportion to my water content, which was at this time 57%, making a total of 41 liters. Tests also indicated, in a form no less categorical and definitive, that I was 22% fat, the same weighing 35 pounds, which went well beyond the normal for a person of my age. To this I had to add the bone and muscle, which weighed 125 pounds and amounted to

78%. In this way, if one adds the 78% on the one hand with the 22% previously mentioned, he accounts for 100% of my body (not all of the first quality), although one should not forget the 41 liters of water that I had distributed through all parts. That was what I amounted to, not more nor less, and so much I could rely on. "The overcoat is another matter," he insisted. The material of the overcoat was, simply, a superficial mantle ("a worm of the mind and as such a parasite," he observed with precision), foreign, like dandruff or the tartar on the teeth (which are not an intrinsic part of the hair on the one hand or of the chewing apparatus on the other). "Pure pathology." An intruder, an uninvited guest that had fastened itself on my skin by way of my brain, which was my chief enemy. "This fabric is not you and must be eliminated by a new living program, a healthy diet, exercises and baths, if you want to save yourself." But, principally, it was indispensable that I stop brooding and adopt a new point of view. "Above all, quit thinking."

For a moment I thought I was going crazy. This "scientific" explanation, expounded with the greatest naturalness in the world and with a wisdom worthy of Amanda, appeared to me like a hallucination to such an extent that I began to suspect (with that lack of faith which characterized me) that it was not the doctor, but I who had done the diagnosis. I was on the point of screaming, and if I didn't do it it was only because the doctor was going to think (not without reason) that I was completely crazy—something which maybe he already suspected. The diagnosis couldn't be mine, nevertheless, because the positive attitude of the doctor was a living contradiction of my inveterate pessimism. He believed (or made me believe, who knows!) that by means of adequate therapy and especially force of will, I ran the best chance of getting rid of those ill-smelling and unhealthy particles that adhered leprously to my skin and, he insisted, "were not mine."

This idea beat against me to the point where I became irritated. How did he know? How was it possible to be so sure that certain matter was part of my body and other wasn't? What reason had he to arrive at the conclusion that that fabric which had incrusted my skin was not as much mine as any liter of water or any pound of flesh, fat or lean? Appraised like beef (and not of the first quality because of the fat I carried), I felt myself besieged by anguish, as if I didn't exist. Those liters of water especially (which I never really did understand) filled me with desperation, and my anxiety was increased when I thought that with the least step I was going to drain away (not even bleeding to death), losing myself down some pipe. Was the overcoat the criminal or was it I who, on becoming an accomplice, helped them eliminate it? Innocent or guilty? It was as if an interior wave were dragging me, sucking me toward another shore, and I, impassive, allowed myself to be carried without putting up the least resistance. In the distance I heard the echo of a voice (possibly Amanda), which was a thread in the air, telling me not to give way to the undertow toward nothingness. As if an attack of panic were overpowering me, I felt claws clutch my chest, knotting the neurons of my brain, squeezing my throat as if I were a professional criminal trained in the best school of death. But in the absurdity of my own perdition, I reasoned still that the particles of wool had been assimilated into my flesh, copulating cellularly with it; they were part of my identity and to eliminate them would be an act of suicide. In this way, obtusely, as if a diabolical force dragged me toward my own annihilation, I insisted on opposing my salvation, thereby lending credence to the theory that the overcoat had tried to kill me, as indeed it almost had, by bringing about the atrophy of my functions—particularly my mental functions.

"It is a question of life or death," interrupted the doctor with a syringe in his hand.

If I allowed myself to be guided by those ideas (which I had not communicated to him, but which he appeared to have right at his fingertips), there was no hope because the only thing I was going to see was the image of myself in the rearview mirror, covered by the overcoat which had traumatized me, he added. I had to destroy *entirely* (he said, underlining the word) that diabolical cancer of my own self-destruction. The diagnosis was elementary, he indicated, and the means whereby the criminal was discovered was unfolded with a simplicity worthy of Sherlock Holmes himself. The image in the rearview mirror was a mirage in the desert that clouded the possibilities of my rebirth. I had to fight against the insidious particles that still were part of me, stuck to my skin like stubborn bloodsuckers.

"Forget the past and start over."

I closed my eyes and felt the prick of the needle.

Subjected to a strict program of physical exercise, that at the same time increased my vitality, I felt the sweat carrying away the remains of the overcoat. I spent two hours a day in the gymnasium to the rhythmic beat of one, two, three, as the calisthenics improved my muscle tone. I exercised day after day, running without going anywhere across the miles which I displaced mechanically on a moving rubber belt which advanced within its own space. I pedalled the vicious circle of bicycle wheels that climbed to the top of imaginary mountains. I lifted weights and the movement of my arms gave back my skeletal image in the mirror as if it were someone else who had shed his oldest skin. The latter tore away like the dry limbs of a tree. The sweat ran from my forehead, dampening my body from head to foot, like a bath that carried with it all the dried rubbish of my body. I would finish doing acrobatics on the parallel bars, leaping onto the long horse and doing turns with the rings. My body was my whole being as I walked a loose cord, maintaining my balance. I would have to leap fences and scale walls in order to prove my dexterity in the face of the new and generous life that had lost its mutilated image. All my unspeakable filth slid away, shriveled, sad, almost melancholy down the drain of the tub in which I took several baths daily. The sponge smoothed my skin, softening and splitting the dryness of the withered crust. In silence and panting to the rhythm of one, two, three, the mutilation took place. My bones, moldy and oxydized, felt the muscular pressure and seemed to squeak, like the hinges of a door that has been closed for centuries. My skeleton bent itself at a waist that had become rotational again. The vertebrae grumbled among themselves and I could hear the snapping of the joints. It was as if bones were united by spiral metal bands that finally expanded under pressure. This produced a pain natural to a limb traumatized by immobility when it finally begins to function normally. But it was a healthy pain produced by an alteration that was the therapy of salvation. I sweated off the scab of my past, training for my own Olympics.

I was growing accustomed to this routine, which gave me a basic feeling of security. I almost overlooked the absence of Amanda, who was waiting for me somewhere outside that immense masonry wall that enclosed the gymnasium. It was as if that activity had a value in itself, free of any ulterior motive, of a goal toward which it was directed. Those exercises were repeated, self-fortifying by their own repetition. There was not the least originality and I came to think that in that abrogation of my individuality lay the essence of a hygiene (a sanitary function) directed toward the elimination of some virus that had nested in my brain. It was an activity as much physical as it was psychological, and in spite of making itself felt by my body (which now held the ego), it demanded a disencumbering which was almost religious, a forgetfulness, as if each joint and pain through exertion, each contraction of the muscles and squeaking of the bones, was saying (I'm afraid I may sound profane, which is not my intention; quite the contrary): forget about yourself, "take up your cross (your body) and follow me."

It was for this reason that I felt disconcerted by my discharge from the hospital, overwhelmed by the news. While I was doing exercises, I didn't have to think, submerged in the mechanics of those hygienic sweats and the co-ordination of muscles, tendons, and bones. I had grown accustomed to the routine of those disciplined hours, to erasing my mind, sunk in the concentrated effort of combat. Besides, I could see progress. I retained, certainly, some bad habits, scabs of the overcoat, dried particles which at times I picked off with my fingernails. But as for the rest, the doctor assured me, what remained was no great thing and I, who had disciplined myself, could take care of it on my own. "In fact, that will be the proof of your complete recovery." I ought not to abandon, of course, those gymnastic exercises, which I should do alone and, so far as I could judge, supervised only by myself. "In this way, if you cast a glance at the rearview mirror, you're not going to be hypnotized," he added smiling, and then closed the door.

There was, of course, the usual paper work, and I remained waiting in my room for some time while all the red tape was taken care of. In reality, I can't say how many hours I was specially prepared in a wheelchair for a discharge which depended on one thing and another. Since I didn't have an overcoat to wear and it was now

146

the middle of summer, I was wearing the clothing I used in the gymnasium: polo shirt, shorts and tennis shoes, which together comprised my entire belongings. I was (relatively) calm, ready to take things one step at a time. But in the depths of my tranquility there beat the bad habits of a hidden unrest which I could only associate with Amanda's absence. From where I sat (without really confessing it) I watched the closed door of the room, expecting from one moment to the next that it would open and Amanda would appear. Because for some reason I thought that Amanda had to arrive without prior word, that she couldn't continue to be a missing person, in spite of an obvious absence to which (with all intention) I have scarcely made reference, perhaps to avoid facing up to a reality that once again could no longer be avoided. Without her (and in this line of reasoning I would accept no argument) I was not leaving this place. In any case, and to make such a course impossible, I cherished the secret hope that for one reason or another some nominal or numerical confusion might render my departure impossible. The least mistake in the number of my hospital insurance (if indeed I had any), for example, some letter more or less in writing my first or last names, a mistake in regard to the date of my birth (that only I knew)—who knew!—would be able to throw a monkey wrench into the decision to release me, obliging me to remain in the hospital (and I trembled only to think of the rearview mirror that would menace me on the other side of the window) from now into the indefinite . . . future.

But it was evident that there was no such intention, and the documentation for my discharge arrived with more efficiency than I might have wished. In opposition to all my calculations, Amanda did not open the door; rather an old humpbacked woman who could scarcely handle its weight and who, nevertheless, did heroic volunteer work by pushing the patients that were ready for release in their wheelchairs. I thought that because of her heroism and precarious physical condition she had been placed there as a model to lift our spirits.

She conducted me down interminable passageways that appeared to cross each other, all equal in a geometric labrynth of entrances and exits that I believed went nowhere. For a while I thought the little old lady was lost (perhaps a worse case than I was) and that it was another patient who was playing the part of volunteer worker. God knew where she was taking me! Alert, I watched her out of the corner of my eye, ready to take off running at the least sign of negligence, restrained only by the thought that she was probably in better condition than I and was not going to let me get away. She rolled me into and out of elevators that went up and down as if no one knew where he was going. We crossed paths with nurses and surgeons with covered faces of a most spiteful and suspicious aspect. The nurses ran hurriedly through the halls, and I could barely see their faces, which they turned away as if wishing to deny me the possibility that one of them might be Amanda. That multitude of medical personnel moved in a mad rush, ready for whatever contingency and cataclysm of the organs, attending sick persons with the most diverse aspects (some of them dead already, probably), dragged on cots or in wheelchairs like mine, saying goodbye to me and see you later. Wasn't it possible that Amanda might be hidden behind some sheet or wrapped in some uniform, half obscured under some headdress? I couldn't get it out of my head that she was going to make her entrance from one moment to the next, but I feared that having changed so much and having gotten rid (almost completely) of the overcoat by which I could be identified, she might go swiftly by without being able to recognize me. I believed, in short, that at any moment I would hear an "Oh, you're here!" that would put a period to our tour of that network of corridors.

Unfortunately, it never happened, and after many stops and starts I found myself at the front door of the hospital. I was set courteously on my feet in the street. Stretching her deformed back and giving me a roguish smile (I understood that it had to do with Helen Hayes forty years after the filming of "A Farewell to Arms"), the old crone who might have made a good blind man's guide, said to me in heavily accented Spanish, "Adiós, amigo." But where was I going to go?

Most certainly, Amanda was not there.

All right, let's be fair and think a moment. Why should Amanda come and look for me or wait for me in that lobby? In reality, she might well have been surprised that something like this had happened. Under normal circumstances Amanda would not be there. To begin with, what right had I to think that Amanda, so clean, would feel obliged to accept my unpleasant odor? Why would she want to go on living with me? It was possible she could have accustomed herself to my stench. If she had accepted it for a time, it must have been from good manners, pure courtesy. Certainly she had remained neat and tidy, as was her custom, and had shied away from me to avoid the contagion of my rottenness. Convinced that my sickness was incurable, she had left me to decay on my own. It was logical, wasn't it? How could she be expected to wait or ever imagine that I had sweated away my crust? To see me there with that "natural" look (polo shirt, shorts and tennis shoes—as if I were an American), there was no way she was going to recognize me, so accustomed was she to my lunacies. To this I had to add a hundred possibilities. In that "Babel of Steel," as they say, "the city that never sleeps," missing persons were common, forming a list of forgotten men who, at most, were a bad luck statistic. If

I had frozen in the park, then I would have come to rest (so Amanda would think) at the morgue, and any further search would have been too much. It was possible also that the little documentation I possessed had been lost, which would have made it impossible for them to tell her I'd disappeared or had been admitted to a hospital (or maybe an insane asylum) where I was merely a number. Perhaps she, for her part, had made fruitless attempts to find me, until finally, giving me up for lost, had followed her star elsewhere. All this and much more might have occurred.

The logic of these arguments terrified me. If I had let myself sink into a physical degradation so contrary to Amanda's nature, wasn't it simply natural that she would have left me? If I had been in a state of absolute mental confusion for an extended period, which now appeared to be the case—calm as I tried to remain—wasn't it possible I might have forgotten incidents that had brought about the final rupture? I had to face up to a fact: I was completely alone and Amanda had abandoned me.

The thought struck me at once as too pitiful and dangerous. Certainly, if that was the truth, I ought to recognize it. Logic demanded it. But the same logic told me that I would go crazy if I accepted such a possibility in so categorical a manner. It was a good idea to consider such a possibility and get ready to accept the worst, trying at the same time to find a solution. Something would turn up. Somehow I would get out of the situation in which I found myself.

With relative confidence I set off on foot, ready to leave the hospital behind me once and for all. If Amanda wasn't here, it was necessary that I should be the one to look for her. Amanda had been an integral part of me for so long that at times we would withdraw to our own private world to commune with each other, leaving a multitude of strangers outside, who were possibly envious. In our union had lain our strength and the breaking of that bond could not be accepted as an ordinary event. The overcoat had also been a stranger to our skins, another enemy in ambush. These arguments made me think that whatever might have been the circumstances of our separation, it was impossible I shouldn't reach the bottom of it. Any rebirth of my being (of our being, perhaps) had to be based on a communion that combined the spirit of the one with that of the other, undisturbed by anything mechanical—including (I affirmed with a vague tremor, as though I might be committing a sin of pride) heavenly mechanics, of which our union was already living proof. If in the past the company of Amanda had been enough to annul the existence of all the rest, serving at the same time to reaffirm me as a person, couldn't the same thing happen now? No, I couldn't resign myself and accept the fact that I was alone . . . forever.

Accompanied by a constellation of galaxies, I began to run. It was the middle of summer and the night was full of stars. There was an intense dry heat, without a breeze, as if the city was also sweating off a scab. Trained as a long distance runner, I launched myself to the four points of the compass. It was as if I ran in a marathon against myself, competing with some other *I* who always grew gradually more distant—the competition of the exorcism. In the distance I seemed to see Amanda as the goal, floating somewhere, in an undefined constellation I had to reach.

Ahead of me, the midnight city was completely empty, a geometrical configuration of buildings made up of the squares and rectangles of doors and windows. On the corners the buildings rose with a heavy verticality, cutting the space like stone knives. Behind me I could hear the distorted cry of someone gripped by hallucinations. I ran through an abstraction of lines, under intermittent neon lights and before the windows of semi-deserted cafes where the seated silhouettes looked like manikins. The sheen of the windows gave back the image of a runner who was myself, superimposing his movements on the rigid forms of men and women, lonely and going nowhere behind the panes of glass and duplicated by interior mirrors. The deserted midnight landscape featured motionless bodies, and the neon lights gave it all the realistic but deathly look of a photograph in which I was the only thing alive. And the starry night gave shape to interplanetary galaxies in constant movement, as if it was part of a dream by Van Gogh in which I was the runner.

The further I ran, the more I realized I was completely in form. I seemed to hear my heart, beating with exact chronological precision. My pulse was an unalterable pendulum which maintained itself at the same level. Oxygen was inhaled and exhaled from my lungs in a rhythm that was almost symphonic. My wild career might have been orchestrated as a *moderato cantabile*. With my gaze fixed on the goal, which was my rebirth, I ran from north to south and from east to west, meanwhile the image in the rearview mirror was broken to smithereens at the edge of the boulevard. Guided by instinct, I remembered something I had written once ("The Case of the Wingless Insects") and the final cry before the curtain fell: "No! I! Amanda!"—the terms of an undeniable equation.

That cry sent a shock of fear through me, without my being able to identify the voice exactly. I had the feeling that somewhere in the foreground was a written sound (which made no sense), consisting of letters, words, punctuation marks. For a moment I thought it was my own voice suddenly denying and affirming itself by means of the pronoun, that linked itself immediately with the name of Amanda, to whom it called—synthesis of a protest. But it could easily be, I told myself, the voice of Amanda, who was at the verge of some mortal peril, crying her own name in order that I might recognize it, a live wire toward which I had to direct myself. Against the geometric configuration of the city, which appeared like a still life painting under the effect of neon lights that were fixed and intermittent at the same time, the voice spoke silently as a graffiti one has to decipher in the catacombs of the subway. Without making a sound, it was a cry painted in a picture, or out of a silent film matched by the subtitle: "No! I! Amanda!" It rang in window apertures, hid behind locked doors, and perhaps this was the reason Amanda had not been able to hunt for me at the hospital. Then everything had an explanation (logical, naturally), because she was under some unknown siege, on the point of being mutilated by a knife that was going to cut her jugular, locked up somewhere and tied to some chair by some sinister criminal. I looked through all the windows of those gigantic buildings, without knowing where the voice was coming from, like a disconcerted "Superman." I tried to identify its point of origin according to its projection across the surface of the asphalt, seeking the angle of incidence of that ray of sound which vibrated in space. But since it was a written cry (a lament of silence), verification was more difficult, as if a time exposure were capable of determining the acoustical angle of a shriek for aid and assistance by means of a blank piece of paper. While running, I practiced the long jump which I had learned in the gymnasium. Confronted by obstacles, I was on the point of falling at every step, and if I didn't do so it was because of the effective training I had received. I practiced the high jump or used a sign post to impel and elevate myself, reaching heights I couldn't have imagined in my wildest dreams. At every moment the dizziness of my marathon increased, without my being able to say where I was and where I was going, headed only toward the final goal, pursuing those words that called me from afar, the echo of some exiled wingless insect on the point of expiring, the absolute synthesis of a present, a past and a future that were united in the three exclamations that were up to some speleologist to decipher. I was bent on an Icarus flight through a moonlit midnight where Amanda and I were trapped.

I searched for a key to it all which, when coupled with the lament, would give me something to hang onto. Like a spiral of celluloid in which intentional cuts have been made, obscuring the meaning, I ran through the city without being able to determine what the script wanted me to do. A passing bird would have seen the skyscrapers of the city without being able to see (or hardly seeing) my wild career through the desolate labrynth of the streets. The detail of some window or some door looming large, with a voice offstage, created a major confusion. The receiving reel of the cry was deliberately out of sync with the silent projection. The aim of the criminal was to disconcert me so that he might thus gain his sinister objective. Because of the changing image, which frequently lost its realistic, still-life quality and went deliberately out of focus, the disorder of my gymnastics increased. For this reason, I would not be able to arrive in time at the place where Amanda was on the point of being dismembered by some dangerous person. It was a time bomb located inside some valise and the tick-tock of the clock marked off precisely the remaining minutes of her life. I was in urgent need of some direction.

Although I had run toward the four points of the compass, the looming presence of the docks seemed to indicate that I had arrived at the extreme southern edge of the city, site of banks, factories and warehouses. Further on, there was only water, the merciless ocean where all runs end and anxieties are drowned. That enemy of the land marked the earth's final point—unless one could walk on water. But I knew that this was impossible (a categorical example of my limitations) and that my steps were numbered, in spite of all those shifts of fortune for which I had trained athletically. I was on the point of returning when, hidden behind the Stock Exchange (naturally), I was able to see a red brick building (with that characteristic color of dried blood), and I recognized that it was the costume factory. A man wrapped in an overcoat, carrying a satchel, came out of the shadows of the deserted street. The clock advanced with its relentless tick-tock (its stroke of midnight, its spiderweb), meanwhile the saboteur rapidly approached the door of the factory and, looking first to one side and then the other, opened the door of the building. It was evident that Amanda must be there, that ignorant of the danger that menaced her (although secretly asking for help by means of those silent exclamatory voices), she back-stitched faces and masks, working a hundred hours of overtime. With a kick I opened the door that the criminal had closed behind him. I ran toward the elevator and watched as the arrow which was indicating one number after another stopped at the seventh floor. I pressed the button and beat uselessly on the door (naturally) because he had intentionally left his door open. Then I went up by the fire escape, leaping stairs while listening to that confusing cry already imaged by the well-known words of "No! I! Amanda!", that indicated danger was near. The spider, meanwhile, with his classic concept of death, wove his web.

It was for this reason, on reaching the seventh floor, I found myself in a labrynth of manikins, as in a horror movie, all equal, the heads inclined toward the sewing machines and surrounded by mirrors (as Orson Wells had been in *The Lady from Shanghai*). In this way the hundred working women were infinitely multiplied, increasing the difficulty of my being able to recognize Amanda. The superimposition of the soundless words below each one of them (as if in a German expressionist film) only made it that much harder and indicated I had to check all of them. At first I began by lifting heads, throwing aside hair that remained in my hand in the case of the badly sewn. At the least contact the limbs (head, trunk, extremities) fell apart on the floor, having become disconnected, and in a few minutes I saw myself surrounded by a hundred corpses. The procedure was definitely wrong and I had to change it immediately. I knew that Amanda was here, crying mutely, gagged perhaps, with adhesive tape on her mouth, feet and hands tied, in some corner. I looked at the clock on the wall and heard the tick-tock of the time bomb hidden in the valise. Realizing I had only minutes left, I had the suspicion that in making me run toward the costume factory they had thrown me off the track, causing me to believe Amanda was here when in reality she was somewhere else. The time bomb had been meant for me, a trick that would have prevented Amanda and me from ever being reunited. I heard the doors of the elevator close and saw that the pointer indicated it was going down. The bomb, consequently, was going to explode any moment. I ran toward the fire stairs, but that door was locked also. The criminal had it all worked out to the last detail and plainly (apparently, I should say) there was no escape.

But, on turning my head, I had to live through an additional terror which, although it might have been a thing of small importance for another, for me was the horror of all horrors. The workers, their faces bent toward their sewing machines, all sewed the same protective coverings: each and every one of them was putting together the overcoat I'd owned. Like the spinners of old, they were weaving the net that was my spiderweb. A perfect geometry outlined itself in space, giving birth to a triangular concept of reality right out of the days of Pythagorus. Only three fixed points were needed to initiate the design. With their indoor loom they made the cloth of the overcoat according to a pattern that was centuries old, waiting for the wingless insect that would serve them as food. Once the work of the straight lines was finished, they began the superimposed spiral, which was their masterwork, each weaver moving in her snail wheel of thread. Terrorized, I felt the weave of the overcoat like an immense tapestry covering all the walls of this loom of death. At the same time, as if a band of singers had recovered the power of speech, but in a twisted voice, a canticle was heard: "No! I! Amanda!" It was as though withered sirens on the heights of some cliff wanted me to lose my way. I was afraid they might lift their heads and that all of them, turned into Amanda, would stop spinning that nightmare, that tapestry of their master art. But a thread unraveled itself, Penelope-like, from one of the weavers of life and began to envelop my bare body, like the cocoon of a caterpillar, anticipating the flight of the butterfly which escapes from the loom of its crime.

In this way, now again in the street, I was able to see the man in the overcoat turn the corner, meanwhile at my back I heard the tick-tock of the rearview mirror, which broke into a thousand pieces.

It was as though yarn from the ball which Amanda had woven into my life, guided me, almost without obstacles, toward the image of the past which had formed the first premise of the syllogism: "we didn't know exactly at what moment during our trip we began to experience those peculiar changes." In this way time broke its chronology (or simply was eliminated) and the montage directed me by an absolute logic toward a source (I thought) of truth. I followed the man in the overcoat, on the look-out for any danger that might lie ahead, but which would be the consequence of what had happened before. As in a film which I had seen years earlier, but which I viewed now in a different way, I opened the door of the apartment and saw the man with his back toward me. The "sequence" had been cut and the area of emphasis changed, giving it a significance it previously lacked, like a scene that is viewed again, after one has seen the end of the picture. Amanda was on the other side of the room. We had to get used to seeing each other with the overcoats on. The apartment was hermetically sealed and the atmosphere was charged. Amanda put on hers (her overcoat) and I mine. Suddenly she looked at him (me) as if, really, she was looking at a stranger, seeing me completely bathed in sweat, but without seeing me in the future, rather in the past that I had begun to fulfill in that moment (before). She appeared not to recognize him (or recognize me) and looked at me (him) with a certain suspicion, as if she feared that from one moment to the next he (I) would take out a dagger (like Jack the Ripper) and do away with her. Since I (that is to say, he) had not taken off the overcoat on entering and remained with it on in spite of the asphyxiating atmosphere in the apartment, she was sure that the man who looked at her had a dagger hidden in the pocket of the overcoat. Actually, he had his hand paralyzed in the pocket and couldn't predict what he was going to do with it. Amanda continued to look at me (him) horror-stuck, and I couldn't interrupt my actions in order to speak to her and calm her and tell her I had returned and that nothing had happened or was going to happen. Galvanized, we saw each other in that first moment of our separation, as if it all had to do with a recurrent nightmare and there was nothing we could do to escape it. The pronoun representing me (I, he) sounded hollow

158

in my head. Then horrified, she, without being able to restrain herself, launched herself toward me, (that is to say, him), toward his arm, yanking it out of the overcoat to see if he had a dagger in the hand that was responsible for our self-annihilation. Disposed to kill her, he actually pulled out the dagger, twisting Amanda's arm in the struggle to free himself, shouting, "No! I! Amanda!"—at last catching sight of me. It was when he turned, wrapped in the overcoat, that we were able to recognize each other, I in the rearview mirror of my past and he in the rearview mirror of his future. Disconcerted on seeing me, he let go of Amanda, who ran toward the back of the apartment, next to the window. I took a leap toward this vision from my past, throwing a left hook which he dodged by jumping backwards, still with the dagger in his hand. Crazily, I threw myself on top of him and the two of us rolled on the floor in a brutal struggle, body to body, while he held the dagger high. By twisting his arm, I succeeded in making him drop it, pinning him with my body, at the same time my left arm managed to reach the dagger he had dropped. The weight of the overcoat obstructed his movements, meanwhile I, more agile, sweating, and freed of that worthless veneer, was able to dominate him. But in the middle of this combat Amanda was caught next to the window and, stumbling, fell backwards into empty air. Catching hold of her tapestry, she appeared to sustain herself in it as she fell through space. Savagely, with the dagger raised on high, enveloped also in that wool I had known so intimately, I began to stab the overcoat over and over, while with my free hand I clutched at Amanda's ball of yarn, which was her tapestry of Ariadne and Penelope, crying (she, I): "No! I! Amanda!"

When I opened my eyes, I still had the shout of the nightmare in my throat. A stewardess leaned toward me, friendly, smiling, somewhat preoccupied.

"Are you feeling ill? Did something happen?"

I had trouble answering her. I was dressed in a suit of brilliant colors, adorned with large showy flowers. She asked me again:

"Is something the matter?"

"No, thank you, it's just that I was sound asleep."

I was, decidedly, on an airplane. All the passengers had gotten off and only the crew remained.

"Rest a moment . . . There's no hurry . . . Take your time," she repeated somewhat mechanically and at the same time looked at me with certain misgivings. "Welcome . . . I hope you've had a good trip."

I shook my head slightly, as if to clear away the heavy dream I'd had, and looked out through the little window, searching intuitively for Amanda, who was waiting for me. I had arrived in a tropical setting of green mountains, blue sky, exuberant vegetation. At the same time I was keenly aware that I was in the midst of a desert, an immense and unlimited desert, all sand, all sun and nameless desolation. It was a tropical desert with a scorching sun, full of beings who vanished into its most merciless and unforgiving landscape. But in that nameless loneliness of iridescent blue sea and pitiless green beauty without end, I saw floating, as I did in my dreams, the desolate form of Amanda. Because through the little window I seemed to see her, under the sun, like a statue which had been waiting for me always, victorious, her gown ruffled by the wind, which had pressed it to her body, the immense waves ready to rise open-mouthed in that desolation . . . Yes, through the little window I seemed to see her in the midst of that nameless desolation . . .

At the same time I saw the sea . . . I tried then to get up and, feeling a dizziness, sat down again in the seat, letting my head fall backwards . . . It was probably the suffocating heat of that desert . . . I closed my eyes and

160

saw the scene, undoubtedly an altar, that I was able to recognize by the chords of the nuptial march: Amanda entered in her wedding dress of classical white lace, white gloves, her arms slightly bent to carry a bouquet of flowers, a veil of tulle, hands united in a certain pose I couldn't describe, herself floating in air, Amanda who evaporated, a crystal rosary that hung down, so very low, there from the heights of a floating figure which never advanced, but retreated into a shell which, when it opened, suggested the Venus of the waters, pagan and naked—she rose divine and Christian, dressed in white and full of grace, the falling tulle and satin, the veil of the bride disappeared in spume . . . Amanda in spume . . . all of her vanished. It had been the constant movement of the sea which had made me giddy and caused me to lose consciousness.

The stewardess leaned over me again, and I smelled a piece of cotton dampened in alcohol.

"If you wish, we can call a doctor . . ."

"No, quite unnecessary," I hastened to say. "I assure you I feel much better now. It must be the heat."

I managed to get up, supporting myself on the back of a seat. The door of the airplane was wide open and there entered through it a boiling, violent brilliance that almost blinded me. The stewardess, carrying my jacket, offered it to me, but only the sight of it was enough to asphyxiate me. I wanted to forget it, I don't know what I told her, possibly no, that it wasn't mine, that it belonged to another passenger . . . And then with all the energy I had left I made my way toward that small door which appeared in flames . . .

The sun struck me in the forehead when I arrived at the door, and I stopped at the top of the stairway. I believed I saw her again in the midst of that sunlight, her wings open in a hope that triumphs in the end . . . Was this, perhaps, finally Amanda? Next to her I seemed to see, in

161

the fullness of that desert covered with burning sands, the two pieces of my baggage ("Of our baggage, you mean") which had returned: those two remote memories left behind, gone, revived from oblivion, undoubtedly confiscated . . . The light, naturally, didn't allow me to see her simply and clearly. Everything was distorted by the glare . . . It was, perhaps, Amanda? It was, perhaps, the return of those two things which had been taken away from us, which had gone away? What should I do, that solitary passenger embarking in the middle of the desert? Was she there, waiting for me in the oven of sand, as if geography and time had never been? Were we strangling at the bottom of the blue iridescent sea that belonged to that exuberant green landscape, that volcanic paradise? Had we reached the submarine depths where the sun never penetrated or were we buried in the sands of that desert, surrounded by a ring of fire? While we advanced towards each other, mirages perhaps, I believed we floated in a fantasy of disintegration—perhaps, just possibly, a disintegration that reunited itself while constantly breaking up. Her bridal veil began to expand as if that tulle were filling everything, along with that lace, in the slow movement of a prolonged dream. The pieces of that body which surged from the luggage on the sand and on the waters, from my head and heart, from the roots of my sex, began to separate themselves. She floated, she whose body went on dividing and opening next to mine, bleeding amidst the tulle and the lace, her hands, thighs, breasts, each and every part of her body. And in a way that seemed to me something like our kisses, our mouths united and separated, met and withdrew, persistent memory, floating in a cosmic tomb . . . Corolla and calyx, reborn or decapitated, I didn't know, Amanda disintegrating like a flower which opened, a disintegrating dream, constantly . . . stamen, anther, filament, stigma . . . pistil, petal, ovule, ovary

162

. . . united again to form . . . I don't know. . . Perhaps the ferocious knife that would pursue me to the last moment . . . implacable focus of a sun bent on wounding me . . . which interrupted me in the pollen of my solitude . . . ? Maybe . . . But no, I rebelled once more . . . But no, I said to myself again and again while I advanced toward her, toward our enigma. She was there at last, magic of our own creation, waiting for me simply, waiting for me eternally, her wings open, affirmative, the gown creased against her body, damp in the wind, boat never sunk in the sea or in the desert.

That was when I looked backward and erased all the pages, destroyed all that I had written, words, all the fantasies of my solitude, of my abandonment. They had been a lie. The pages blazed, the words of my deception, I myself creator of the fiery circle that burned around me, or would go on to be the only and final reality which surged, phoenix-like, from the ashes of my own words.

About the Author

Matías Montes Huidobro is currently a Professor of Spanish at the University of Hawaii, where his prolific pen encompasses all the genres. Recent publications include two plays, one in *Cuban American Theater* by Arte Publico Press and the other in *Cuban Theater in the United States: A Critical Anthology* by Bilingual Review Press.

About the Translators

John Mitchell and Ruth Mitchell de Aguilar are a father and daughter team whose first collaboration, José Rubén Romero's *Notes of a Villager*, was published by Plover Press in 1988. John is the winner of a Pushcart Prize for his collection *Alaska Stories* and Ruth a full-time resident of Mexico for the last twenty-two years, where she runs a weaving shop in Pátzcuaro, Michoacán.

DUE DATE

			Printed in USA